# Clara Stitched in Secrets

A SWEET HISTORICAL ROMANCE

KERRI KASTLE

KERRI KASTLE

Copyright © 2024 by Kerri Kastle

All rights reserved.

No portion of this book may be reproduced in any form without written permission from the publisher or author except as permitted by U.S. copyright law.

# Contents

1. Chapter One — 1
2. Chapter Two — 12
3. Chapter Three — 25
4. Chapter Four — 35
5. Chapter Five — 44
6. Chapter Six — 54
7. Chapter Seven — 66
8. Chapter Eight — 78
9. Chapter Nine — 88
10. Chapter Ten — 97
11. Chapter Eleven — 105
12. Chapter Twelve — 113
13. Chapter Thirteen — 126
14. Chapter Fourteen — 136

| | | |
|---|---|---|
| 15. | Chapter Fifteen | 144 |
| 16. | Chapter Sixteen | 158 |
| 17. | Chapter Seventeen | 170 |
| 18. | Chapter Eighteen | 181 |
| 19. | Chapter Nineteen | 197 |
| 20. | Chapter Twenty | 203 |

# Chapter One

Clara Mills had done many questionable things in her twenty-two years of life, but sneaking into a grand ball through the servants' entrance while wearing a stolen—*borrowed*, she corrected herself—mask definitely topped the list.

Her heart thundered against her ribs as she slipped through the back door of Pembroke House, careful not to snag her midnight blue gown on the rough wooden frame.

The dress was another one of her "borrowed" items for the night, rescued from a client who'd deemed it unfashionable after one wearing.

Clara had spent three nights transforming it, and now no one would recognize the once-plain gown with its newly added silver embroidery and delicate beading.

*Just like no one recognizes the seamstress behind Madame Celestine's creations*, she thought with a mixture of pride and irritation.

The mask she wore—a masterpiece of silver filigree and blue silk that had cost her three sleepless nights to perfect—felt both like armor and a prison.

Protection from discovery, yes, but also a constant reminder that she didn't belong in this glittering world she'd been skirting for the past five years.

*Fix Lady Pembroke's dress and leave,* she reminded herself firmly. *No lingering, no dreaming, no—*

"Watch where you're going!" A harried footman nearly collided with her, his arms full of fresh flowers.

Clara pressed herself against the wall, inhaling the mingled scents of beeswax candles, roses, and excitement that always seemed to perfume these grand events. So different from the lavender and cotton that scented her tiny shop in the unfashionable part of London.

Her fingers tightened around her sewing kit—the same battered leather case she'd had since she was sixteen. Back then, she'd been nothing but a seamstress's apprentice with callused fingers and impossible dreams.

Now she was... well, still a seamstress with callused fingers, but one whose creations graced the finest ballrooms in London. Even if she had to pretend to be French to make it happen.

The servants' corridors buzzed with pre-ball chaos. Maids rushed past with trays of champagne, footmen hauled ice sculptures, and somewhere nearby a butler was having what sounded like an absolute fit about the wrong vintage being served.

Clara navigated through it all with the ease of someone who'd spent more time below stairs than above them.

*Five years,* she mused, ducking into an alcove to let a line of footmen pass.

Five years since she'd first had the mad idea to reinvent herself as the mysterious Madame Celestine. She'd been seventeen, desperate, and tired of watching her designs being claimed by her employer.

The French accent had been an impulsive addition—after all, who would trust an English girl barely out of her teens with their finest gowns?

But it had worked. Oh, how it had worked.

"Madame Celestine!" Lady Pembroke's urgent whisper cut through her reminiscing. "Thank heavens you've come!"

Clara turned to find her latest client half-hidden in a side chamber, clutching what appeared to be a significant amount of torn silk.

*Right then. Time to work some magic.*

She squared her shoulders, adjusted her mask one final time, and glided forward with all the confidence of her alter ego. Time to be the miracle worker they all believed Madame Celestine to be.

Even if her hands were shaking slightly within her gloves.

Lady Pembroke yanked Clara into the side chamber with surprising strength for someone wearing what appeared to be half the silk in London. "Look at this disaster!"

Clara assessed the damage with practiced eyes.

The tear in the cornflower blue silk was substantial—running a good six inches along the side seam—but nothing she couldn't fix. She'd repaired worse damage in less time, usually while some society lady wept dramatically nearby.

"How did this happen?" Clara asked, already reaching for her needle and thread.

"That horrible little dog of Lady Ashworth's! The beast caught my skirts as I was coming down the stairs and—" Lady Pembroke made a ripping gesture that sent her bracelets jangling.

Clara bit back a smile.

She'd met Lady Ashworth's "horrible little dog"—a perfectly sweet creature who probably just wanted attention. Much like its owner.

As she worked, her quick fingers weaving invisible stitches through the delicate silk, fragments of conversation drifted in from the hallway.

"Can you believe Eustace Montague actually came?"

"The Duke hasn't attended a ball in months..."

"Still brooding over that Italian fiancée..."

Clara's hands never paused, but her ears pricked up.

Everyone knew about the Duke of Ravencroft and his broken engagement—it had been last season's favorite scandal. She'd heard all about it while fitting gowns for gossiping ladies.

*Poor man*, she thought, then immediately corrected herself. *Poor rich, handsome duke with his enormous estate and broken heart. However does he manage?*

"Stand still, my lady," she murmured as Lady Pembroke fidgeted. "Just one more minute."

Working quickly but carefully—because rushed stitches were obvious stitches, as her first teacher had drilled into her head—Clara finished the repair. She sat back on her heels, surveying her work with critical eyes.

Perfect. Not even she could spot where the tear had been.

"There," she said, knotting the final stitch. "Good as new."

Lady Pembroke twisted to examine the repair in a nearby mirror. "Magnificent! You truly are a miracle worker, Madame Celestine." She clasped Clara's hands. "You simply must join the ball as my guest. I insist!"

*Say no*, her sensible side urged. *Get out while you can.*

But through the chamber's window, Clara caught a glimpse of the gardens. Moonlight silvered the paths and turned the fountain's spray to diamonds. Music drifted in—a waltz, her favorite. And for just a moment, she allowed herself to imagine...

*Don't you dare*, the practical voice in her head warned. *Remember what happened last time you got carried away with dreams?*

She should leave. She had three gowns to finish, a rent payment due, and absolutely no business pretending to be anything other than what she was—a working woman with a gift for needle and thread.

But oh, how beautiful it all looked. Just one small taste of the world she spent her life adorning others for...

"You're already dressed for it," Lady Pembroke coaxed, gesturing to Clara's gown. "And that mask is simply divine. Your own work, I assume?"

Clara touched the mask self-consciously. Three nights of work, yes, but worth every pricked finger and lost hour of sleep. The silver filigree caught the light just so, and the blue silk perfectly matched her eyes—not that anyone would see them behind the mask.

"Just for a moment," she whispered, more to herself than to Lady Pembroke. "What's the worst that could happen?"

Five years of careful planning, of building her reputation stitch by stitch, of being the mysterious Madame Celestine who was never seen at social events... and she was about to risk it all for one dance in a moonlit garden.

*This is madness*, that sensible voice insisted. *You shouldn't!*

And she really shouldn't, Clara thought to herself.

"Thank you, my lady, but I must decline." Clara curtsied, gathering her sewing kit. "I have other appointments this evening."

But as she slipped out of the chamber and headed for the servants' exit, the glimpse of those moonlit gardens through every window she passed made her steps slow.

Just one peek couldn't hurt, could it? The gardens were technically outside the ball... and she'd always wondered what the famous Pembroke roses looked like up close...

*No, no, absolutely not*, she scolded herself, even as her feet carried her toward the garden door. She'd just take one quick look and then—

"Oof!"

She collided with what felt like a wall of solid muscle, her sewing kit tumbling from her hands. Strong hands steadied her before she could fall, and she found herself staring up into the most striking green eyes she'd ever seen.

"My apologies," said a voice that sent shivers down her spine. "I wasn't watching where I was going."

Clara meant to step back. She really did. But those hands were still on her waist, and something about his half-smile made her feel wonderfully dizzy.

"Clearly not," she managed, proud that her voice came out steady. "Do you always lurk in doorways waiting to assault unsuspecting ladies?"

His eyebrows shot up, and that half-smile grew into something devastatingly charming. "Only on Tuesdays. And only the particularly intriguing ones who appear to be escaping the ball rather than entering it."

"I'm not escaping," she protested. "I'm... taking air."

"In the opposite direction of the gardens?"

Clara felt her cheeks heat. Thank goodness for the mask. "Perhaps I prefer my air without roses and judgmental gentlemen."

He laughed—a rich, warm sound that did dangerous things to her resolve. "Then allow me to make amends. The gardens really are spectacular, and I happen to be an excellent guide. Not judgmental at all, I promise."

*Say no*, that sensible voice screamed. *Leave now!*

"I shouldn't..." she began.

"Ah, but the best stories never start with 'I should,'" he pointed out, offering his arm.

And maybe it was the moonlight, or his smile, or the way this whole evening felt like a dream anyway, but Clara found herself taking his arm.

"Just a brief tour," she stipulated.

"Of course." His eyes sparkled with mischief. "Though I should warn you—the gardens have a way of making time slip away."

As he led her down the moonlit path, Clara tried to remind herself of all the reasons this was a terrible idea. But with his warm hand covering hers on his arm, and the night air sweet with roses, those reasons seemed to slip away just as easily as time.

"I'm Eustace, by the way," he said softly.

"Charlotte," she lied, picking the first name that came to mind. She'd regret it later, but right now, in this moment, she just wanted to be someone else. Someone who could walk in moonlit gardens with handsome strangers without worrying about rent payments and reputations.

"Well, Charlotte," he smiled down at her, "shall we see if we can find some trouble to get into?"

Clara knew she should be scandalized by such a suggestion. Instead, she found herself laughing. "I thought you promised not to be judgmental?"

"I did. Which is why I'm not judging your clear desire for adventure."

"You know nothing about me."

"I know you're wearing a mask that cost someone many sleepless nights to create. I know you move like someone who's used to going unnoticed, yet you hold yourself like a queen. And I know that despite your protests, you're just as curious as I am to see where this evening might lead."

Clara's heart skipped. He was far too perceptive. "For someone not judging, you're making an awful lot of assumptions."

"Not assumptions. Observations." He paused by the fountain, turning to face her. "Dance with me?"

Music drifted from the ballroom, a waltz that made her feet itch to move. "There's no one else dancing out here."

"Precisely why we should."

*Don't*, that sensible voice begged. But Clara was already stepping into his arms, her heart racing as his hand settled on her waist.

After all, what was one dance in a moonlit garden? What could possibly go wrong?

Eustace was an excellent dancer. Of course he was.

Clara tried not to notice how perfectly they moved together, how his hand felt warm and sure against her waist, how his eyes never left her face.

"You're very quiet suddenly," he murmured, guiding her around the fountain.

"I'm concentrating on not falling into the water."

"I wouldn't let you fall." His voice had dropped lower, more intimate. "I suspect you rarely let anyone catch you though, do you?"

Clara's breath caught. He was far too perceptive, this stranger who wasn't really a stranger anymore. "You talk as if you know me."

"I'd like to."

The music from the ballroom changed then, shifting to a slower, more romantic melody that made her heart ache. Violins and piano intertwined in a way that seemed to echo the strange tension building between them.

"Come inside," Eustace said softly. "Dance with me properly."

"I shouldn't." But her protest sounded weak even to her own ears.

"Even mysterious ladies in masks deserve to dance sometimes." His thumb traced small circles on her hand. "Just one more dance. Inside, where I can see your eyes properly."

*This is the stupidest thing you've ever done,* her sensible side warned as she let him lead her toward the ballroom. *Stupider than the French accent. Stupider than—*

But then they were through the doors, and Clara forgot how to think entirely. The ballroom was a swirl of candlelight and color, hundreds of crystals in the chandeliers casting rainbow shadows across the floor.

Whispers followed them as Eustace led her to the center of the room.

"Who is she?"

"Have you ever seen her before?"

"Look how he's looking at her..."

Clara's heart thundered as Eustace pulled her close again. This wasn't like the garden. Here, under the bright lights and curious stares, everything felt more intense.

More real.

"Everyone's staring," she whispered.

"Let them." His hand slid slightly lower on her back, just shy of scandalous. "I can't blame them. You're the most interesting thing that's happened all season."

They moved together as if they'd been dancing for years. Each turn, each step perfectly matched.

Clara felt almost dizzy with it—the warmth of his hands, the scent of his cologne, the way the room seemed to fade until it was just the two of them.

"Tell me who you are," he murmured, his lips close to her ear.

"I can't."

"Can't? Or won't?"

She looked up at him then, a mistake. His eyes held hers, intense and searching, and something electric passed between them. He pulled her incrementally closer, their bodies now touching in ways that would definitely set tongues wagging.

"Both," she managed.

The music swelled, and Eustace spun her in a series of quick turns that left her breathless. As they turned, Clara caught glimpses of the crowd—wide eyes, pointing fingers, furious whispers.

And then—it happened so quickly—her mask caught on a button of his coat during a turn. She felt the ribbon give way before she could stop it.

Time seemed to freeze.

The mask fell.

Gasps echoed through the ballroom.

"My God," someone whispered. "It's her. It's Vittoria."

Clara's blood ran cold. Who?

But then she saw Eustace's face—the shock, the recognition, the flash of something else she couldn't name—and realized exactly who they thought she was.

The countess. His former fiancée.

Before she could speak, before she could move, before she could do anything to correct this horrible mistake, Eustace's voice rang out clear and strong:

"It seems the fates have decided to give us another chance, my dear."

The room erupted in excited chatter. Clara stood frozen, her heart pounding so hard she thought it might burst. This couldn't be happening. This wasn't—

But it was. And as Eustace lifted her hand to his lips, his eyes never leaving hers, Clara had one crystal clear thought:

*I am in so much trouble.*

# Chapter Two

Good grief.

Eustace Blackwood, the Duke of Ravencroft, glared at the invitation on his desk as if it had personally offended him.

*Another ball invitation in just three days.*

*Another evening of desperate mamas throwing their smiling daughters at him.*

*Another waste of his precious time.*

*He had a lot of things he would rather do with his time.*

"No," he said firmly, not even looking up at his mother who stood in the doorway of his study. "Whatever you're about to say, Mother, the answer is no."

"Darling, you haven't attended a single social event in months." His mother's voice carried that particular tone of patience that meant she wouldn't leave until she got her way. "People are starting to talk."

"Let them talk." He picked up his pen, pretending to focus on the estate ledger before him. "I have more important things to do than watch young ladies pretend to swoon in my direction."

"You're the Duke of Ravencroft."

"Really? I had forgotten."

"Eustace." The sharp note in her voice made him look up.

His mother, usually the picture of aristocratic composure, actually looked worried. "I'm concerned about you. Ever since the... incident with the countess—"

"Don't." His voice came out harder than intended.

He sighed and softened it with effort. "Mother, please."

She moved into the room, her silk skirts rustling. "You can't hide in this study forever. The ton is beginning to wonder if you've gone mad. Lord Pembroke actually asked me if you'd taken up residence in a monastery."

Despite himself, Eustace felt his lips twitch. "A monastery might be peaceful."

His mother glared at him. "One evening, son." She placed her hand on his desk, and he noticed the fine tremor in her fingers. "Just attend the ball at Pembroke House. Make an appearance. Show society that the Duke of Ravencroft hasn't completely lost his senses."

Eustace ran a hand through his dark hair, disturbing what his valet had carefully arranged that morning.

He hated seeing his mother worried.

Hated even more that she might be right—he had been hiding.

And what gentleman wouldn't hide this season?

"I have heard there will be the dimmest of lights. The darkness will help," she added hopefully. "You won't have to talk to anyone you don't wish to."

"That's not—" He stopped, sighing. "Fine. One hour. I'll make an appearance, bow to the right people, and leave before anyone can corner me into a dance."

His mother's face lit up. "Thank you, darling. Though perhaps if you did dance with someone—"

"Don't push it," he growled, but there was no real heat in it.

After she left, Eustace leaned back in his chair, scowling at the ceiling. He'd gotten soft.

The old him would never have given in so easily.

But lately... lately he'd felt restless. As if something was missing, though he refused to acknowledge what that something might be.

It definitely wasn't marriage, though. Anything but that.

Marriage was a trap.

Love was an even bigger one. He'd learned that lesson four years ago when his arranged engagement to Countess Vittoria had fallen apart.

She'd been everything a proper lady should be—quiet, demure, and utterly boring.

The thought of spending his life with someone who could barely hold a conversation had been suffocating.

He had needed more and ran from all the proper ladies he met.

He didn't want proper, that much was clear.

But he also didn't know what it was he wanted.

Growing up a duke meant he hadn't been allowed to mix with different types of people as his friends had. He had no idea that a lady could be anything other than proper.

Yet here he was, agreeing to attend another blasted ball where everyone would be watching him, whispering behind their fans about the duke who'd broken his engagement and retreated from society.

"One hour," he muttered to himself, standing to ring for his valet. "What's the worst that could happen?"

Hours later, as he adjusted his black coat and descended from his carriage at Pembroke House, Eustace was already regretting his decision.

The sound of music and laughter spilled out into the night, making his teeth clench.

Inside would be a sea of people all wanting something from him—his title, his fortune, his hand in marriage.

But he was the Duke of Ravencroft, and Ravencrofts didn't break their word. Even if they desperately wanted to.

From the corner of his eyes, he glimpsed a female sneaking in through the back of the estate, a bag in her hands. She had a mask on.

A thief? No. A thief would not wear such a beautiful dress. So, who was she?

He shrugged. None of his business.

"One hour," he reminded himself again, squaring his shoulders and mounting the steps. "Just one bloody hour."

He had no way of knowing that in less than that time, his carefully ordered world would be turned completely upside down by a mysterious woman in the garden who was nothing like the quiet, proper lady he remembered—and everything he'd never known he wanted.

***

Eustace had barely stepped into Pembroke House when the vultures descended.

"Your Grace!" Lady Makeral materialized at his elbow, dragging what appeared to be her fourth eligible daughter. "Have you met my Prudence?"

He hadn't, nor did he want to.

But he offered a stiff bow anyway, already scanning for an escape route.

"She plays the pianoforte," The Lady continued, beaming. "And speaks three languages."

"How... accomplished." The word tasted like ash in his mouth.

He'd heard the same thing about at least fifty other young ladies this season.

It only got worse from there.

By the time he'd made it halfway across the ballroom, he'd been introduced to no fewer than seven potential brides, each more insipid than the last.

He caught bits of their mothers' desperate pitches as he moved through the crowd.

"...excellent housekeeper..."

"...very obedient..."

"...comes with a substantial dowry..."

Good God. Were they selling horses or daughters?

His cravat felt too tight.

The air too thick.

Lady Pembroke had decorated every available surface with roses, and their cloying scent was giving him a headache.

Or perhaps that was just the endless parade of simpering debutantes.

"Your Grace!" Another mama was heading his way, this one towing twins in matching pink gowns.

No. Absolutely not.

Eustace turned on his heel and strode toward the garden doors, ignoring the disappointed sighs in his wake.

Let them talk. Let them whisper about the antisocial duke.

He didn't care.

The cool night air hit his face like a blessing. He breathed deeply, letting the tension ease from his shoulders. Out here, with only the moon and stars for company, he could almost forget the suffocating expectations that came with his title.

He was just considering whether he could get away with spending the entire hour in the garden when he rounded a corner and collided with someone.

He apologized, ready to run off again, but her reply stopped him short.

She stood in a pool of moonlight, and for a moment Eustace forgot how to breathe.

Her gown was the color of midnight, studded with tiny crystals that caught the light like stars. But it was her hair that caught his attention—pale gold, almost silver in the moonlight, tumbling in elegant waves from beneath her mask.

The mask itself was a work of art, all delicate silver filigree and blue stones that matched her gown. But it was her mouth that held his gaze—full lips curved in what might have been amusement or challenge.

And as they talked, Eustace wondered what was wrong with him.

He didn't flirt. He didn't engage. He certainly didn't stand in moonlit gardens exchanging meaningful looks with mysterious masked women.

But when she tilted her head, studying him with eyes that sparkled behind her mask, Eustace found himself taking a step closer, drawn by something he couldn't—or wouldn't—name.

He had no idea who she was. In a society where he knew everyone's name, title, and family connections going back three generations, this woman was a complete mystery.

And for the first time in years, Eustace Blackwood, Duke of Ravencroft, found himself intrigued.

***

An hour later, Eustace was shocked over and over again.

He remembered when her mask had slipped after their dance, and time had seemed to stop at that moment.

Eustace remembered staring like a fool, his world tilting on its axis. That face. He knew that face.

*Vittoria Romano.*

The crowd around them had frozen, whispers rising like a tide. He could hear the shock, the speculation, the hunger for scandal in their voices.

And beneath it all, he saw the panic in her eyes—eyes that looked so familiar yet somehow different from what he remembered.

He didn't think.

He had just acted.

"Countess Romano, my dear former betrothed," he said, his voice carrying across the suddenly silent ballroom. "I believe this reconciliation is long overdue."

The words fell from his lips before he could stop them.

But seeing the absolute shock and fear flash across her face, he wondered if he'd made the right choice.

Better to control the narrative than let the ton tear them both apart with speculation and ruin both their reputations.

Besides, anything was better than another evening of desperate mamas throwing their daughters at him.

But as he stood there, watching color drain from her cheeks, memories washed over him...

*"Eustace!" Six-year-old Vittoria had squealed, chasing him through the Romano estate's garden. "Wait for me!"*

*He'd slowed his steps, letting her catch up. At ten, he'd felt so grown-up, so responsible for his little betrothed.*

*She'd been sweet then, always following him around with wide eyes and endless questions about England.*

The memory shifted, darkened...

*"Countess Romano," he'd said years later, bowing over her hand at a ball.*

*She'd been seventeen then, he twenty-one.*

*Gone was the curious little girl. In her place stood a proper lady who spoke only when spoken to, who never lifted her eyes from the floor.*

*A lady he didn't know.*

*"Yes, Your Grace," she'd murmured to every question he asked.*

*"No, Your Grace," to any suggestion of activity more exciting than needlework.*

*"As you wish, Your Grace," when he'd tried to draw her into conversation about books, politics, anything.*

*It had been like talking to a particularly well-dressed wall.*

*The final straw had come during their last meeting before he broke the engagement. He'd found her in the library, hoping to finally have a real conversation.*

*"What do you think about the new trade agreements with France?" he'd asked, desperately wanting to reconnect with the little girl who had made his heart soar.*

*She'd blinked at him. "I think whatever you think is best, Your Grace, I'm but a woman."*

*He'd wanted to scream.*

But this woman... this Vittoria...

Eustace studied her now, trying to reconcile his memories with the sharp-tongued creature who'd just spent the last hour trading witty barbs with him in the garden.

Who'd challenged his opinions on Shakespeare. Who'd made him laugh—actually laugh—with her cutting observations about Lord Pembroke's new wig.

She held herself differently too.

Gone was the demure slouch, the downcast eyes.

This Vittoria stood straight, met his gaze directly, carried herself with a confidence he'd never seen before.

This Vitoria wasn't proper at all.

What had happened in the last two years to change her so completely?

And why did he find himself hoping she'd never change back?

"Your Grace..." she said now, and even her voice was different—stronger, clearer, with a hint of something he couldn't quite place. "I shall have to take my leave now," and she started to sneak away.

He offered his arm automatically, hyperaware of every whisper, every stare that followed them.

"Not now, Vittoria," he said. "The world is staring at you now, you can't just leave yet."

*Plus, I need to figure out what the devil is going on*, he added silently.

She glared at him. "I don't care if people are staring! I need to get out of here!"

Oh, something was definitely going on. People didn't change this dramatically without reason. The shy, proper, utterly boring Vittoria he'd known would never have dared to quirk an eyebrow at him the way she was doing now.

"Well, I'm sorry, my lady, but this isn't Italy. The ton here will tear you apart."

"Italy?" She asked incredulously. "Well, how generous of you to help me."

Eustace felt his lips twitch despite himself.

Generous indeed. More like selfish.

Because now that he'd found someone who could actually hold a conversation—who could make him smile—he wasn't about to let her disappear back to wherever she had come from.

Even if she wasn't quite the Vittoria he remembered.

Especially because she wasn't the Vittoria he remembered.

\*\*\*

*Caught you!* Eustace thought with a grin as he caught sight of her silk skirts as they disappeared around the hedge maze's corner and quickened his pace.

She had excused herself to right her dress but knowing the very younger Vittoria he had been obsessed with, he knew it was a ploy.

And it was. He almost laughed as he followed after her escaping figure.

She wanted to leave him here?

For a woman who'd spent the entire ball captivating the ton, she was certainly in a hurry to vanish before anyone saw her.

He actually laughed now, the sound still foreign.

"Lady Vittoria," he called out, his deep voice carrying across the dew-dampened grass. "Or should I say... Charlotte?"

She froze, her shoulders tensing beneath her elaborate gown—one of exceptional craftsmanship.

When she turned, the dying moonlight caught the defiant tilt of her chin. "Stop following me!" she snapped, and he shook his head.

"I can't leave you alone now, can I? Our fate has been entwined even if you lied to me about your name, Lady Charlotte."

She scoffed. "You can hardly blame me for using a false name when you were the one who turned our brief garden encounter into a public reconciliation without asking me how I felt about it!" Her voice carried a sharp edge he'd never heard from Vittoria before.

The Vittoria he remembered had barely spoken above a whisper.

He narrowed his eyes. "Well, you used to care only about what I felt and never what you felt... why has that suddenly changed?"

She gaped at him, confused. "What? Why would I—you know what, I blame you for all of this."

He grinned, seeing the frustration in her eyes. "You can hardly blame me for wondering why my former betrothed introduced herself with a false name." He closed the distance between them, studying her face. The resemblance was uncanny, yet... "Though I must say, you've developed quite a sharp tongue since our last meeting."

She stuttered for a movement as if she had no idea how to respond. Then she lifted one elegantly arched eyebrow. "Perhaps you simply never bothered to listen before."

The retort caught him off guard—another surprise from a woman who'd once been as predictable as a church sermon. Every interaction tonight had left him increasingly unsettled.

This wasn't the meek Italian contessa who'd bored him to tears with endless discussions of weather and embroidery.

"Stay at my estate," he found himself saying, the words emerging before he'd fully formed the thought.

"I beg your pardon?" She blinked rapidly, taking a small step backward.

"You need accommodation while in London, and after tonight's... announcement, it would be expected." He moved closer, oddly pleased when she stood her ground this time. "Unless you'd prefer to explain to the ton why you're staying elsewhere?"

"I hardly think—"

"It's perfectly proper. My mother and sister are in residence." He noticed how she tensed at the mention of his family but filed that detail away for later consideration. "Though I must admit, I'm curious about your convenient appearance tonight. Four years of silence, and suddenly..."

She lifted her chin higher. "If you're implying something, Your Grace, do speak plainly. I don't understand your words."

"Plainly?" He couldn't help the sardonic smile that curved his lips. "Very well. When I mentioned our betrothal years, you didn't reminisce. When Lady Hampton asked about your family's palazzo in Venice earlier, you changed the subject. Rather odd behavior for someone who spent her entire childhood there, wouldn't you say?"

For a fraction of a second, something like panic flashed in her eyes before she masked it with cool dignity. "P-Perhaps I simply prefer not to dwell in the past?"

"Perhaps." He drew the word out, watching her closely. "Or perhaps there's another explanation entirely."

She met his gaze steadily, but her fingers worried the edge of her fan. "I don't require accommodation, Your Grace. I'm perfectly capable of—"

"I insist." He offered his arm, noting how she hesitated before taking it. "After all, what kind of gentleman would I be if I didn't look after my... reconciled betrothed?"

Her fingers tightened almost imperceptibly on his arm. "You're impossible."

"So I've been told." He guided her toward his waiting carriage, increasingly certain that something wasn't adding up—and increasingly determined to discover what it was. "Though I must say, you're nothing like I remembered."

"People change, Your Grace."

"Indeed they do." He helped her into the carriage, catching a whiff of lavender—not the expensive Italian perfume Vittoria had favored, this one was something... wild. He loved it. "Though rarely quite so... comprehensively."

As the carriage pulled away from Pembroke House, Eustace settled back to study the woman across from him.

She was a puzzle, this sharp-tongued, quick-witted version of Vittoria, and despite his general disdain for society and its games, he found himself oddly eager to solve it.

Even if, as he suspected, the solution might prove more complicated than he imagined.

# Chapter Three

Clara stared at the ceiling of her lavishly appointed guest room, counting the cherubs painted there for the hundredth time.

One more hour. Just one more hour until the servants started their morning routines, and she could slip away unnoticed.

She hadn't slept a wink. How could she?

The events of the ball kept playing through her mind like a fever dream. The dance, the mask falling, everyone thinking she was the countess... and worst of all, Eustace's pronouncement about fate giving them another chance and announcing reconciliation.

*Fate isn't giving anyone anything except a massive headache*, she thought, throwing off the silk covers.

The grandfather clock in the hallway chimed four times.

Perfect.

The kitchen staff would begin work soon, providing just enough commotion to cover her escape. She'd already packed her small bag—not that she'd unpacked much to begin with, it was only her sewing kit she'd left in the gardens. How it had ended up in this room, she didn't know.

This "stay" was never meant to last.

Clara pulled on the simplest dress in the closet, the one least likely to rustle. She'd done enough sneaking around grand houses to know every creak could be fatal to a good escape.

Her fingers fumbled with the buttons as she remembered the way Eustace had looked at her last night—not with the cold politeness she'd expected from a duke, but with genuine interest.

*Stop that*, she scolded herself. *He's not looking at you. He's looking at someone else entirely.*

She grabbed her bag and pressed her ear to the door. Silence. Now or never.

The hallway stretched before her like a tunnel of judgment, all gilt frames and ancestral portraits staring down their painted noses at her. Clara could swear one particularly stern-looking duchess followed her with disapproving eyes as she tiptoed past.

*I know, I know*, she thought at the portrait. *I don't belong here. That's why I'm leaving.*

Three steps down the grand staircase, and a board creaked. Clara froze, heart in her throat.

Nothing.

Two more steps. Another creak.

"Going somewhere?"

Clara's heart stopped. She knew that voice. Had danced to its warm tones just hours ago. Had been trying very hard not to think about it since.

She turned slowly, clutching her bag like a shield. There stood Eustace, looking unfairly handsome for such an ungodly hour, leaning against the banister with an expression of mixed amusement and curiosity.

*Of course he's awake. Of course he caught me. Because why would anything in this disaster of a situation go right?*

"I was just..." Her mind raced for an excuse. Any excuse. "Going for an early morning... walk?"

Even to her own ears, it sounded pathetic.

"A walk." His eyebrow arched. "With all your belongings?"

"I like to be prepared?" Clara winced at how her voice lifted at the end, making it sound like a question.

"For what? A surprise voyage to the Continent?"

Despite her panic, Clara felt a spark of that defiance that always got her into trouble. "Perhaps I'm practicing for when pirates commandeer the house. One can never be too prepared for such things, wouldn't you agree?"

A smile tugged at his lips. "Absolutely. Though I don't recall any pirates being quite so stealthy about their exits."

"Well, clearly you've never met a proper lady pirate."

*Stop bantering with him!* her sensible side screamed. *This is not helping!*

But Eustace was already descending the stairs, that infuriating half-smile still playing on his face. "Come on, my sneaky friend. If you're up, you might as well join me for an early breakfast. We can discuss your apparent need to practice for natural disasters."

Clara opened her mouth to refuse, to insist she really did need to leave, to finally tell him the truth—but her stomach chose that exact moment to growl. Loudly.

Eustace's smile widened. "I'll take that as a yes."

And somehow, despite all her careful planning, Clara found herself following him toward the breakfast room, her escape plan thoroughly and utterly foiled.

Well, she thought resignedly, *at least this day can't get any worse.*

She really needed to stop thinking things like that. The universe seemed to take them as personal challenges.

\*\*\*

Clara's hopes of a quiet, private breakfast evaporated the moment they entered the morning room.

Apparently, early rising ran in the Montague family. Eustace's mother, the Dowager Duchess, sat regally at the table, while his younger sister, Lady Margaret, was curled in a window seat with a book.

Both women looked up with identical expressions of delighted surprise.

*Wonderful*, Clara thought. *An audience for my humiliation.*

"Vittoria, darling!" The dowager rose, arms outstretched. "We didn't expect you until later!"

Clara's stomach churned as the older woman embraced her. The dowager smelled of lavender and warmth, exactly how Clara had always imagined a mother should smell. The guilt twisted deeper.

"I'm an early riser," she managed, trying not to stiffen in the embrace.

"Just like when we were children!" Lady Margaret abandoned her book and practically bounced over. "Do you remember those summer mornings in Florence? We'd sneak out to watch the sunrise from Papa's orangery?"

Clara's heart stuttered. *Here we go.* "That was... quite some time ago."

"Oh, but surely you remember!" Lady Margaret's eyes sparkled with nostalgia. "You used to bring those delicious pastries from that little bakery near the cathedral. What were they called again?"

*Think fast, think fast.* Clara opened her mouth, not sure what would come out—

"Darling," Eustace cut in smoothly, "perhaps we might let our guest eat before we overwhelm her with childhood memories?"

Clara shot him a grateful look before remembering she wasn't supposed to be grateful to him for anything. He'd gotten her into this mess in the first place.

The breakfast table looked as if it had been set for a small army. Clara's mouth watered at the sight of fresh bread, eggs, and what looked like honeycomb dripping onto a silver plate. When was the last time she'd had honey?

"You're so thin," the Dowager observed, watching Clara butter a piece of toast. "Don't they feed you properly in Italy?"

"Mother," Eustace warned.

"I'm simply concerned! A lady needs her strength." The Dowager passed a plate of eggs. "Especially if there are... celebrations to plan."

Clara choked on her toast. Eustace's hand appeared with a glass of water, which she accepted without thinking.

"It's rather early for matchmaking, isn't it?" Eustace's tone was light, but Clara heard the warning in it.

"Nonsense! It's never too early to discuss happiness." The Dowager beamed at Clara. "And we were all so happy when you arrived last night. Like fate itself had intervened."

*More like disaster intervened*, Clara thought, gulping more water.

Lady Margaret leaned forward eagerly. "Will you tell us about the latest fashions in Florence? I hear the styles this season are simply divine."

Now this, finally, was territory Clara could navigate. She might not know anything about Florence's orangeries, but she knew fashion like she knew her own heartbeat.

*Just get through breakfast*, she told herself. *Then you can figure out how to untangle this mess.*

She had no idea the mess was about to get so much bigger.

"The silhouettes this season," Clara began, finding comfort in familiar territory, "are moving away from the Empire waist—" She caught herself. "Though of course, you'd know all about that from your recent visit to Milan, Margaret."

Lady Margaret blinked. "Oh! Yes, of course..."

Clara pressed her advantage. "What did you think of the new sleeve treatments? Personally, I find the Italian interpretation far more elegant than the French versions."

The Dowager chimed in, her tone eager. "Yes, tell us, *did* you find those deep hues popular there? I've heard the Italians favor much bolder colors!"

Clara nodded, seizing the opportunity to lean into her fabricated persona. "Indeed, there's a vibrant jewel-toned palette trending. It's as if the very landscape of Florence influences the gowns—the emerald greens of the hills, sapphire blues echoing the Tuscan skies, even the rich red wine hues." Clara's words flowed smoothly now, weaving truth and invention together as seamlessly as one of her own creations.

Every gown she'd crafted for Italian clients, every snippet of gossip she'd heard about Florence's fashion houses, every detail she'd memorized from fashion plates—she poured it all out now, building a vision of Italy from threads of silk and imagination.

Lady Margaret hung on every word, enraptured. "Oh, it sounds enchanting!"

Just then, she piped up with an innocent smile. "And do they still adore the florals? Mama said you loved flowers as a child."

Clara froze for the briefest second, her heart lurching in her chest.

She quickly forced a light laugh, drawing on every ounce of composure she could muster. "Florals are quite timeless, aren't they? But in Italy, I'm particularly fond of camellias—" *Thank you, Madame Celestine's client notes,* she thought, grateful she'd once sewn an entire dress inspired by camellia blossoms for an Italian noblewoman. "There's something rather romantic about them, don't you think?"

She glanced at Louisa and quickly added, "Though not nearly as lovely as the gardens here in England, of course."

The dowager nodded approvingly, distracted by the charming description. "How poetic! Perhaps we should visit Florence next summer, Margaret."

But Margaret wasn't entirely satisfied. She tilted her head, studying Clara with youthful curiosity. "I suppose Florence must feel so different after all this time away, doesn't it? Do you miss it?"

Clara's chest tightened.

She forced a wistful smile, casting her gaze downward as if lost in thought.

"Oh, Florence will always hold a special place in my heart. But... London too has its charms." She threw a quick, subtle glance toward Eustace, hoping he might deflect this line of questioning.

As if on cue, Eustace leaned back, crossing his arms with a slight smirk. "Well, now that we're all experts on Italian fashion, perhaps we might ask our guest to stay long enough to convince the rest of us to dress in Florentine finery?"

A small, grateful smile tugged at Clara's lips, but she played along, lifting her chin with an air of jesting defiance.

"I'll have you know, Your Grace, Florence's style has been declared the height of elegance. But," she tilted her head with a playful glint in her eyes, "some of us might be too hopelessly British to keep up."

Everyone laughed, and the moment passed, but Clara knew she'd only narrowly escaped. Her stomach churned as she navigated yet another question, aware that with each word, she was spinning herself deeper into the web of this deception.

The Dowager nodded approvingly as Clara described the latest innovations in silk-weaving. "You've become quite the fashion expert, my dear. So different from the shy girl who used to hide behind her sketching papers."

*If you only knew,* Clara thought, taking a fortifying sip of tea.

"Speaking of changes," Lady Margaret piped up, "you seem so... different now. More..."

"Opinionated?" Eustace supplied, earning himself a glare from Clara.

"Confident," Lady Margaret finished. "It suits you."

The genuine warmth in her voice made Clara's chest ache. These people were so ready to welcome back their long-lost friend, and here she was, deceiving them all.

"Perhaps we should discuss the real reason for this reunion," Eustace said suddenly, setting down his cup with careful precision.

Clara's heart stopped.

This was it. He'd figured it out.

He was going to expose her right here, in front of his family, and—

"I think we should announce our engagement."

Tea splashed across the pristine tablecloth as Clara's cup clattered against its saucer. "I beg your pardon?"

"It makes perfect sense," he continued, as if he hadn't just casually suggested something absolutely insane. "Society already expects it. Your return is the talk of London. We might as well make it official."

The Dowager clasped her hands in delight. "Oh, how wonderful!"

"Absolutely not." The words burst from Clara before she could stop them.

Silence fell over the breakfast table like a heavy curtain.

"Perhaps," Eustace said carefully, "we should discuss this privately."

"There's nothing to discuss." Clara stood so quickly her chair scraped against the floor. "You can't just... just... decide these things!"

"Can't I? We were betrothed before."

"That was—" *Different. With someone else. A complete disaster in the making.* "—a long time ago."

Eustace rose too, his height suddenly intimidating. "Exactly why it's time to set things right."

"Set things right?" Clara laughed, a slightly hysterical sound. "Nothing about this is right!"

"If you'd just listen—"

"No, *you* listen." She jabbed a finger at his chest, manners forgotten. "You can't just announce engagements over breakfast like you're ordering more tea! That's not how this works. That's not how any of this works!"

She was causing a scene. She knew she was causing a scene. The Dowager's shocked face and Margaret's wide eyes told her exactly how much of a scene she was causing.

But she couldn't stop. All the panic and guilt and confusion of the past day boiled over, and suddenly she was storming out of the breakfast room, her half-eaten toast forgotten.

"Vittoria, wait!"

"My name is—" She bit back the truth just in time. "—not important right now!"

She ran. Up the stairs, down the corridor, back to her borrowed room where nothing made sense but at least she could breathe.

*I have to tell him*, she thought, pressing her forehead against the cool door. *Tonight. I'll tell him tonight.*

She had no idea that by tonight, things would be even more complicated than she could possibly imagine.

# Chapter Four

Eustace Montague, the Duke of Ravencroft, slouched in his study, glaring at the roaring fire as if it had personally insulted him.

Well, he had been glaring at everything like it was an insult to him since breakfast with Vittoria.

The mere idea of convincing a woman—his former betrothed from an engagement that he himself had broken—to enter into some sort of sham engagement gnawed at his pride.

Eustace hated the entire institution of marriage and the relentless matchmaking that seemed to cling to him like a shadow wherever he went.

Since inheriting his title, he'd been stalked by fortune-hunting mamas and their daughters, all fluttering about like colorful, shrill birds trying to nest.

Four years ago, he had been told that Vittoria cried when he broke the engagement.

So that meant she had wanted to marry him, like every other available noblewoman.

So why? Why was she so... different now?

Any other female might gasp at first but would definitely agree to his proposal.

Instead, this woman who couldn't even look into his eyes four years ago had stared at him like he was mad as she rejected his proposal.

And it irritated him more than he cared to admit.

The garden encounter and her revealing afterward had caught him off guard. Just the memory of her dark eyes, sharp and observant under her mask, stirred something in him.

She hadn't simpered, hadn't giggled, hadn't been the timid lady he remembered.

Instead, she had looked right at him with an unwavering gaze, bold enough to match his own.

Her smile hadn't been the vacant, practiced sort he'd come to expect, either; it had been the kind of smile that hinted at secrets, as though she knew something he didn't.

And that—more than her beauty—was what stayed with him.

There was a quick wit in her that intrigued him, even though he'd rather eat his own cravat than admit it to anyone.

But he needed her to agree to this ruse, and that need rankled.

The fact that she was so different now made her practically a stranger, and the idea of opening himself up, even a fraction, to persuade her set his teeth on edge.

He wasn't the kind of man who let others in easily. He valued his solitude—his cold, quiet home that allowed him to escape the frivolous whirl of society.

This arrangement was supposed to keep people out of his life, not invite them in.

Eustace rubbed a hand over his face, thinking back to the last time he'd let anyone close.

Three years ago, he'd still been young and foolish, full of the sort of ideals that only life could beat out of a man.

After Vittoria. He thought he'd found the one.

Her name was Lara, the daughter of a baron he'd met during his early days in London. She'd been a vision, with dark hair and a laugh that made him think the world was a brighter place than he'd realized.

He'd really thought she might be the one—until he'd discovered that she'd been interested only in his title and wealth.

When he'd confronted her, she hadn't denied it; she'd even laughed, as though his heartbreak was amusing. "Oh, Eustace," she'd said lightly, "I thought you understood how the world works."

After that, he'd sworn off marriage. Women were trouble, and he would never again let his heart—or his pride—fall victim to someone else's whim. Since then, his focus had been on his estate, his responsibilities, and keeping society at arm's length.

And now, here he was, preparing to ask Vittoria to do the very thing he'd sworn off. She could ruin everything if she wanted to—she was an unknown, a wild card.

But somehow, despite himself, he trusted her in a way that didn't make sense. He could see from their brief encounter that she was as much of an outsider to this world as he was, and that sparked a strange sort of sympathy within him.

She was like him, bound by the expectations of others yet fighting to stay free.

He rose, pacing the room, hands clasped behind his back. Why did the thought of her intrigue him so?

Vittoria had an air about her—quiet strength, a confidence that came from somewhere other than a title.

The way she'd met his eyes in the garden, unafraid and unapologetic, had stirred something he hadn't felt in years. He found himself remembering how the moonlight had glanced off her hair, how her voice had sounded low and soft, as if she was sharing a secret meant only for him. And the worst part? He'd liked it.

Eustace grimaced, feeling the tightening in his chest. This was ridiculous.

She was supposed to be his shield from society's clutches, not some woman he spent his nights thinking about. He despised the fact that his mind kept returning to her, replaying every moment of their meeting, every word exchanged.

Even now, he could almost hear her voice, that calm, collected tone that had hidden something fiery underneath. He didn't like mystery, but she was one. And he wanted to solve her, to uncover the secrets she so carefully guarded.

But first, he had to convince her. Eustace knew he couldn't be gentle about it. A direct approach was best. He wouldn't flatter her or play coy. No, he would be blunt, as he was with everyone. He'd try again, tell her exactly what he needed from her, and if she didn't like it, well, that was her problem, not his.

Or at least, that was what he told himself as he steeled his resolve, forcing down the strange twinge in his chest.

***

Hours later, Eustace sat in the private lounge of White's, staring at the thin smoke drifting up from his glass of brandy.

Across from him, Monsieur Dubois—a Frenchman with a knack for good business but a tendency to prattle on endlessly—was enthusiastically discussing the logistics of their latest investment venture.

Eustace nodded at the right times, keeping his face impassive, his thoughts drifting back to the absurdity of his current situation.

Here he was, the Duke of Ravencroft, considering a fake engagement with a woman who was both captivating and infuriating, a woman he had once rejected, just to get society off his back.

His mind was still partially on Vittoria when he spotted Lord Edmund, who had just slithered into the room like the snake he was.

Eustace's jaw tightened at the sight of his rival. Edmund Blackthorne had been a thorn in his side for years, trying to edge his way into Eustace's business dealings, smearing his name whenever possible.

And here he was again, strolling over with that smug look on his face.

"Ravencroft," Edmund drawled, ignoring Dubois and pulling a chair close. "I hear congratulations are in order. Quite a sudden reunion with your dear Vittoria, isn't it?"

Eustace didn't bother with a welcoming expression. He only raised a brow, his voice as flat as he could make it. "What do you want, Blackthorne?"

Edmund's smile widened as he glanced around the room, ensuring they weren't overheard. "I'd think you'd want to be careful, Eustace. Don't want to get too cozy with a lady whose origins are… questionable."

"Speak plainly," Eustace snapped, though he felt an uneasy chill creep up his spine. He wasn't about to give Edmund the satisfaction of showing it.

"Oh, I would, if I didn't enjoy watching you struggle," Edmund said, leaning back with an air of satisfaction. "But let's just say that

I happen to know your charming fiancée has more in common with needle and thread than with any noble blood."

Eustace's fists tightened under the table, but he kept his face unreadable. He felt a surge of irritation and absurdity in his veins.

Edmund was always stirring up nonsense; this was just his latest attempt. "You expect me to believe that Vittoria—a woman I've known all her life, whose family is well-known across Italy—isn't who she says she is?"

Edmund leaned forward, a smug look glinting in his eyes. "I'm saying she isn't Vittoria at all.

Rather, she's something far less... respectable. The name Clara Mills or Celestine the French seamstress ring any bells?"

Eustace held back a snort, making a show of swirling his brandy. "Clara Mills," he repeated. "You've finally lost your mind."

"Oh, perhaps," Edmund said, his tone amused. "But I think you know better than to dismiss me, Eustace. You may have convinced the rest of London that you've brought back the lost countess, but I know what I know. And I'm going to prove it."

Eustace's eyes met Edmund's, his gaze as cold as stone. "If you think you can scare me with some wild story about a seamstress, think again. Vittoria is under my protection, and any attempt to slander her will end badly for you."

Edmund gave a mocking little laugh, shaking his head as though Eustace had said something amusing. "You're a fool, Eustace. A loyal fool, but a fool all the same. She's a fraud, and by the time I'm through, everyone will know it. Including the court, if it comes to that."

Eustace's irritation turned to something harder, sharper. He wasn't about to let Edmund ruin everything he'd carefully planned with his stupid lies. "Leave her alone, Edmund," he said, his voice low and dangerous. "You'll keep your nose out of this, or I'll make sure you regret it."

Edmund's smile didn't falter, though there was a flash of something darker in his eyes. "Careful, Duke. It's not a threat if it's the truth. The truth has a way of coming out, no matter how hard you try to bury it."

With a final smug smile, Edmund rose, smoothing his jacket before strolling off, clearly pleased with himself. Eustace watched him go, jaw clenched tight enough to crack. He'd faced off with Edmund countless times, but this—this was a new low, even for him.

As he leaned back, staring at the empty seat across from him, Eustace's mind drifted to Vittoria again. She'd been on his mind constantly, from the night in the garden to the moment she'd looked at him with those dark, challenging eyes.

He didn't know what to believe, but he knew one thing: he wanted her, even if it was reckless. Even if it went against everything he'd ever promised himself.

If Edmund had his way, it would all be ruined. But Eustace wasn't about to let that happen. Not for himself, and certainly not for her.

\*\*\*

Eustace waited in the quiet drawing room of his estate, his arms folded across his chest as he stared into the low, flickering fire.

He'd sent for Vittoria an hour ago, and it felt like an eternity had passed.

Edmund's smug words rang in his ears, and for the first time, a sliver of doubt had wedged its way into his mind.

His instincts screamed at him that Edmund's accusations were pure nonsense, yet he couldn't ignore the way his rival had spoken about her, the certainty in his tone.

When the door finally opened, and she stepped in, he straightened, watching her every move. She looked surprised to see him alone, a faint wariness in her eyes as she took him in.

There was something in her expression—something too guarded, too careful—that made him uneasy.

"Your Grace," she said with a graceful dip of her head, but he could sense her tension. It mirrored his own.

He didn't waste time with pleasantries. "Lord Edmund Blackthorne, my business rival, paid me a visit at the club today," he began, his voice cool and measured.

He saw her swallow, her fingers twisting together for the briefest moment before she stilled them. "Lord Edmund?" she repeated, as if unsure where this was leading.

"Yes. He had... interesting things to say." Eustace took a step closer, never breaking eye contact. "About you, specifically."

Her composure slipped, just a fraction, but enough for him to notice. He watched the way her breath hitched, the way her face seemed to pale ever so slightly. It was that tiny, involuntary reaction that sent another sliver of doubt through him—a feeling he despised. "He claims you aren't who you say you are," he said softly, almost accusingly. "That you're not Vittoria Romano at all."

She held his gaze, but he saw the tremor in her stance, the hint of panic flitting through her eyes. "What do you think?" she asked, her voice just above a whisper.

The question threw him off guard, though he refused to let it show. What did he think? He'd spent his entire life trusting himself and no one else, priding himself on his instincts. And yet, looking at her now, he realized he didn't know. The woman before him, the one who had so easily caught his attention, had made him question himself in ways he didn't like. But goodness, he was drawn to her—no matter who she really was.

He narrowed his gaze, choosing his words carefully. "I think," he began slowly, "that I don't like being made a fool of. I also know I've known you all your life. You could never lie to me."

Her face went white, and he saw her jaw clench as if she were gathering the strength to speak. She opened her mouth, then shut it, her gaze dropping for the first time since she'd entered the room.

She looked up at him, her expression resigned. "Very well, you do know me well," she said, her voice barely above a murmur. "I'll agree to your terms. The engagement... we can proceed with it as you suggested."

He blinked, taken aback by her sudden compliance. He hadn't expected her to give in so quickly, especially after the defiance he'd seen in her eyes before.

"You're agreeing?" he asked, not even trying to mask his surprise.

"Yes." Her voice was steady, though he could see the tension in her shoulders. "I'll do as you ask."

He studied her, a strange mixture of relief and frustration simmering beneath the surface. She was an enigma, one he couldn't quite grasp. And, as much as he hated to admit it, he was relieved that she would stay, even if only as his temporary fiancée. This arrangement might be built on lies and pretense, but he found himself wanting her near, drawn to her despite every rational thought that screamed at him to stay away.

# Chapter Five

Clara paced the length of her guest room, fingers twisted in her skirts, her mind a jumble of worry and strategy.

She could hardly believe the corner she'd painted herself into. Pretending to be an Italian countess, agreeing to a fake engagement with a duke—*what would the ladies at her shop who demanded Madame Celestine say*? They'd either laugh her right out of the workroom or clutch their pearls.

Yet, here she was, facing the truth head-on. If her identity slipped now, the fallout would be disastrous.

No amount of stitching or clever needlework could patch up a ruined reputation.

The ton would cast her out; her stepfamily would delight in her failure. She'd be nothing more than a scandal, whispered about and shunned.

*Alright, Clara,* she told herself, taking a steadying breath. *You've gotten out of tighter situations.* She looked around, feeling the weight of her decision settle.

If Eustace wanted a fake engagement, well, that could be manageable. And she'd keep it just that—fake. She had no desire to entertain any more of his haughty "I'm above it all" attitude than necessary.

Her lips curved into a sly smile as she remembered their exchanges so far.

He might be a duke, but she had plenty of fire herself. And *she* knew how to handle a needle and thread, to create magic out of fabric—*he* just knew how to create scandals.

"Arrogant man," she muttered, tapping her fingers against her side.

Yes, Eustace had made it clear he wasn't looking for love, and that suited her just fine. She wouldn't let herself be charmed by that maddening smile or the way he held himself like he owned the world.

*No, thank you.*

With a determined nod, she settled on her plan. She'd be the perfect faux fiancée, graceful and poised, as untouchable as the finest silk. And when it was all over, she'd slip back into her real life as seamlessly as she'd slipped into Vittoria's. She'd be back to her quiet, sensible world, her secrets intact.

It wasn't what she wanted, but it was the only way forward.

Clara took a slow breath as she walked down the corridor to the drawing room where Eustace waited.

She was still steeling herself for this conversation, aware that she'd need every ounce of composure—and her sharpest tongue—to deal with whatever terms the duke had in mind.

The door was half-open, and she could see him standing by the fireplace, looking every bit the picture of effortless nobility. His dark coat was immaculate, and that infuriating confidence radiated from him as he sipped his tea like he hadn't a single worry in the world.

She straightened her shoulders and entered, chin held high. Eustace looked up, one brow arching as she took a seat across from him without waiting for an invitation.

"Well, good evening to you too," he said, amusement flickering in his eyes.

Clara folded her hands neatly in her lap. "Let's skip the pleasantries, shall we? If we're going to go through with this... arrangement of yours, I'd like to get a few things clear."

His smile was subtle, but she could tell he was enjoying this—probably too much. "By all means," he said, leaning back with a casual elegance that made her want to roll her eyes. "Ladies first."

*Alright then.* She narrowed her gaze, feeling her determination bubble up. "Firstly, this engagement—this *pretend* engagement," she emphasized, "will be purely practical. No... grand gestures in public, no... declarations of undying affection."

His eyes gleamed, and for a moment she thought he was going to laugh. "So, no candlelit serenades or bouquets of roses, you mean?"

"Yes, precisely." She kept her face calm, though a part of her was itching to match his sarcasm with a cutting remark. "And no attempts to... win my heart or some such nonsense," she added, lifting her chin a little higher, even as she felt her cheeks warm at the thought.

To her surprise, Eustace let out a chuckle. "Believe me, Vittoria, that's the last thing you'll need to worry about."

*Well, that's a relief,* she told herself, though her pride prickled at how quickly he dismissed the possibility.

She'd been the one insisting on keeping things formal, yet something about his assuredness made her feel oddly... stung.

"Good," she replied, mustering all the casualness she could. "That's settled, then."

Eustace took another sip of tea, eyes never leaving hers. "And in return, I expect the same from you. No sudden bouts of romantic attachment, no tearful confessions, and certainly no attempts to reform my supposedly rakish ways."

Clara's lips twitched as she fought back a smile. "I assure you, Duke, that task is far too hopeless for me to waste my time on."

"Excellent." He gave her a look of mock approval. "You're much more sensible than I expected."

For a split second, she almost laughed—but then she remembered exactly why she was here, and that this wasn't a game.

*This is your future,* she reminded herself, *and it's all riding on this ridiculous arrangement.*

The amusement faded from her face. "So, what exactly will we be telling people?" she asked, leaning forward slightly. "How are we explaining our sudden... reconciliation?"

Eustace's expression shifted, his gaze calculating as he considered her question. "We'll keep it simple. I'll say that upon meeting you again, I found you... changed. Much improved from the Vittoria I once knew."

Clara arched a brow, stifling a snort. "Much improved? How flattering."

He shrugged, a smile flickering at the corners of his mouth. "Would you prefer I say 'remarkably matured'?"

*This man and his arrogance,* Clara thought, shaking her head. "Whatever you like," she replied with a sigh. "So long as you don't make it sound as though I threw myself at you in some desperate bid to reignite a long-lost flame."

Eustace gave her a look, his eyes gleaming with a hint of a challenge. "Trust me, that thought never even crossed my mind."

Something in his gaze made her pulse race, though she refused to let it show. Instead, she crossed her arms, keeping her expression cool. "Good, because I have no interest in that sort of spectacle."

He nodded, his smile fading slightly as he looked at her thoughtfully. "Then we're in agreement. We'll present a dignified, calm front. Let society assume whatever it will, so long as it leaves us alone."

Clara nodded.

This, at least, was something she could agree to.

No entanglements, no romantic illusions—just a straightforward plan with a beginning and an end. And as long as they both played their parts right, perhaps she really could slip back into her life when all this was over.

Yet as she met his gaze across the room, she couldn't shake the feeling that nothing about this would be as straightforward as she was telling herself.

The tea had long grown cold on the table, but Clara barely noticed. She was too busy focusing on every word Eustace spoke, her mind calculating the next step, the next word, the next way to steer this entire tangled mess in her favor.

She was a seamstress, after all—practical to her core.

And this was just another skill to hone, she told herself, like any new stitch or pattern.

Eustace cleared his throat, drawing her attention back to him. "Then let's establish the final terms. Six weeks. We'll make the announcement soon, and after that, we're bound to attend several social engagements together."

Clara felt a slight jolt at the word "announcement," but she held her expression neutral.

"Six weeks. Agreed," she said. "And if at any point I need to... discreetly excuse myself from any of these engagements?"

Eustace's eyes flickered with something close to amusement. "Afraid the ton might prove too dull?"

"Afraid I might need to escape a bit sooner than planned, yes." She met his gaze evenly, unwilling to let him think she was intimidated. "It's been a... whirlwind of an experience so far."

"Ah," he replied, a knowing glint in his eyes. "Then I'll do my best to make it bearable for you."

*Bearable*. Clara swallowed a laugh.

Here she was, being offered "bearable" by a duke who wanted nothing more than a convenient bride, and yet... wasn't she in the same predicament? She needed this arrangement as much as he did, if not more.

"Another thing," she said carefully, choosing her words. "While we're... engaged"—the word still felt foreign in her mouth—"I have a reputation to maintain. I won't have you spreading tales about your fiancée behind closed doors."

Eustace chuckled. "Rest assured, Vittoria, I've no intention of dragging your name through any mud. My goal is to keep our reputations intact—not scandalize them further."

She felt a prick of annoyance at his self-assurance, though it was oddly reassuring, too. "And one more thing," she added, watching him carefully. "I reserve the right to end this entire charade if I find myself... inconvenienced."

He leaned back in his chair, eyes narrowing just slightly. "Ah, so you reserve the right to break the agreement at will?"

"Just as you do, I'd assume," she countered, lifting her chin. "If you've any doubts about me—"

"You know," he interrupted, a gleam of challenge in his eyes, "I must say, I find this 'fiancée' of mine rather... demanding."

"Only because I've no interest in letting you—or anyone else—take advantage of me, Duke." Clara's tone was sharp, though inwardly she felt a pang of something she couldn't quite name. She wasn't just fencing with words anymore; she was wrestling with her own pride and the faint flicker of something dangerously close to... trust?

For a moment, they sat in silence, the weight of their mutual caution heavy between them.

Finally, Eustace spoke, his voice quieter but firm. "Very well. You have my word that I'll respect your boundaries. But, " he added, a slight smirk returning to his lips, "you should know, the ton loves a good romance. A bit of... affection in public might be necessary."

*Affection?* Her heart skipped, her mind racing at the thought. "Define... affection."

"A hand on your arm, a few dances together," he replied smoothly, watching her with amusement as though he could read every thought passing through her mind. "The occasional touch, to make it convincing. Unless, of course, that troubles you?"

Clara fought to keep her voice steady. "Not at all. I'm a professional, Duke. I'm sure I can manage a bit of *acting*."

Eustace's smirk widened. "Good to know. Then we're agreed."

She forced herself to nod, though her pulse thrummed in her ears.

It would be fine—she'd stay composed, act her part, keep things perfectly practical.

No feelings, no mess, and absolutely, *absolutely* no falling for the Duke of Ravencroft.

It was as simple as sewing a perfect seam.

Or so she tried to tell herself.

As Clara rose from her chair, the reality of it all weighed on her shoulders like one of Lady Pembroke's overembellished ballgowns.

She had just agreed to a six-week engagement to the Duke of Ravencroft. Six weeks of keeping her secrets locked tight, of pretending to be something—someone—she was not.

Eustace walked her to the door, his expression a blend of satisfaction and calculation, as though he'd just sealed a profitable deal. "One more thing, Vittoria. If anyone questions you about our relationship, I'd recommend a touch of enthusiasm. We wouldn't want our engagement to seem too... tepid, would we?"

Her mouth twitched into something that might've resembled a smile if it weren't laced with sarcasm. "Don't worry, Your Grace. I'm sure I can muster a bit of admiration for such a... *charming* fiancé."

He chuckled softly, a warm, rolling sound that she did *not* find attractive. Not at all. "I'll look forward to seeing this admiration on display, then."

Clara kept her face impassive, though a ripple of irritation danced through her.

The man was infuriatingly smug, and far too sure of himself.

But this was her last chance to keep her life intact, and so she gave him a polite, if faintly barbed, nod. "Consider it done."

As she turned to leave, Eustace reached out, his hand lightly catching her wrist. She stopped, the touch startling her, and turned back to find his expression softened, unreadable.

"If anyone—especially Edmund—questions you, come directly to me," he said quietly. "If we're going to do this, we do it together."

The words, unexpectedly kind, made her feel like a thread had been pulled from a tightly sewn seam.

She was acutely aware of the warmth of his hand on her wrist, the hint of sincerity in his eyes.

But before she could linger too long on that feeling, she reminded herself who he was: the Duke of Ravencroft, a man who saw this engagement as little more than an inconvenience to be dealt with.

She stepped back, breaking the contact. "Of course, Your Grace. I'll be sure to let you know if I need... *help*."

He gave her a curt nod, a flicker of something unreadable in his gaze before he turned, leaving her to step into the corridor alone.

***

As Clara walked down the hallway, the grand portraits lining the walls stared down at her, regal and disdainful, as if reminding her of how absurd this all was.

Who was she to walk these halls as though she belonged? She was Clara, seamstress, not some grand lady with a title and a legacy to protect.

But as she took each step, she straightened her spine, gripping the edges of her skirts in tight fists.

She might not be born to this, but she would wear this disguise as well as any gown she had stitched together.

Downstairs, a cluster of footmen scurried to and fro, preparing the house for some grand affair she could only guess at.

She caught a few glances in her direction, polite but curious, as though she were a new piece of furniture they were trying to decide how to place.

It struck her just how many eyes would be on her in the coming days—not just these servants, but the whole of London society.

"Fake fiancée to a duke," she muttered under her breath. "Clara, you have really outdone yourself this time."

The thought of seeing Eustace's smug face at every social event, of pretending to swoon at his every word, made her stomach twist with irritation.

But beneath that, there was a faint thrill she couldn't quite squash. She would never have been invited into this world otherwise, and for all the dangers, it was still a world of opulence and glamour that fascinated her.

As she finally stepped outside, the cool morning air cleared her head a little, and she took in a deep breath, savoring the sharpness of it.

She had six weeks to play the role of Eustace's fiancée, six weeks to keep her head down, blend in, and emerge unscathed. She would pull it off with all the precision and poise she brought to her work. She *had* to.

Because for Clara Mills, failure wasn't just inconvenient. It was the end of everything she had fought for.

## Chapter Six

Eustace Blackwood prided himself on maintaining control in all circumstances.

Yet as he escorted his supposed fiancée through the corridors of his estate, he found his carefully constructed walls crumbling with each click of her heels against the marble floor.

"The east wing should suit your needs," he said curtly, keeping a proper distance between them despite the maddening urge to draw closer. "It's private enough to avoid gossip, yet close enough to my quarters to maintain appearances."

He wondered if his sudden overwhelming attraction for her was a punishment from the heavens for how he'd broken their engagement all those years ago.

Vittoria tilted her head, studying the corridor with an appraising eye that seemed more housekeeper than aristocrat. "The lighting is excellent," she murmured, more to herself than to him. "Though these curtains could use replacing—the silk is wearing thin at the seams."

Eustace's steps faltered. Since when did Vittoria Romano, the pampered Italian countess he'd known two years ago, notice such mundane details?

The woman beside him was a contradiction wrapped in silk and secrets.

The Vittoria he remembered had been demure to the point of dullness, this Vittoria's eyes sparkled with barely contained wit.

How had she changed so drastically in five years?

"Here," he said, perhaps more gruffly than necessary, pushing open the double doors to her suite. The morning light streamed through tall windows, illuminating the cream and gold decor his mother had selected years ago.

Vittoria stepped inside, and Eustace found himself watching her reaction with inexplicable intensity. She moved through the space like she was cataloging every detail—not with the entitled air of a countess examining her domain, but with the practical assessment of someone who understood how a household ran.

"The dressing room could be rearranged," she said, gesturing to the adjoining chamber. "If we moved the armoire to that wall and adjusted the mirrors, it would create better flow for—" She stopped abruptly, color rising in her cheeks.

"For what?" Eustace pressed, stepping closer than propriety strictly allowed. The scent of lavender and something indefinably *her* teased his senses.

"For... moving about in grand gowns," she finished lamely, taking a step back that brought her against the wall.

Eustace knew he should maintain his distance. This arrangement was meant to be temporary and purely practical—a way to silence society's gossip and his mother's endless matchmaking.

Yet he found himself following her retreat, one hand coming to rest against the wall beside her head.

"Strange," he murmured, studying her face for answers to questions he hadn't even formed yet. "I don't recall you being so... knowledgeable about household matters in Italy."

Her throat worked as she swallowed, but her gaze remained steady. "People change, Your Grace."

"Indeed they do." His other hand rose of its own accord, fingers hovering near but not quite touching the curve of her cheek. "You've become quite... unexpected."

A knock at the door shattered the moment. Vittoria slipped away from him like smoke, leaving Eustace's hand pressed against cool wallpaper where warm skin should have been.

"Your Grace?" His butler's voice carried through the door. "The housekeeper requires your approval for the weekly menus."

Eustace straightened, adjusting his cravat with perhaps more force than necessary. "I'll be there shortly," he called out, then turned back to Vittoria.

She stood by the window now, sunlight catching the auburn highlights in her white-blonde hair—another difference from the golden blonde he remembered.

"I trust you'll find everything to your satisfaction," he said stiffly. "Ring for anything you need."

She nodded, a ghost of a smile playing at her lips. "Thank you, Your Grace."

He strode from the room before he could do something foolish, like demand answers to the questions multiplying in his mind, or worse, taste that maddening smile for himself.

The breakfast room, when he entered it an hour later, was flooded with morning light that did nothing to improve his mood.

Vittoria was already there, deep in conversation with his sister Margaret about the household accounts of all things.

Since when?

"The kitchen expenses could be managed more efficiently," Vittoria was saying, her finger tracing a line in the account book. "If you order certain staples in bulk during—" She broke off as she noticed him, that becoming flush coloring her cheeks again.

"Don't let me interrupt such thrilling discourse," Eustace drawled, dropping into his chair with deliberate casualness. The footman approached with coffee, and he noted how Vittoria thanked the man by name—Thomas—with a warmth that spoke of genuine regard rather than condescension.

Every little thing she did only added to the puzzle she presented.

The way she automatically adjusted her napkin to protect her gown from stains, her practiced grace in handling the delicate teacup, the unconscious way she noticed when a servant's cup needed refilling—all spoke of someone intimately familiar with both sides of the social hierarchy.

"I hope you found your rooms satisfactory," Margaret said, breaking into his thoughts.

"Oh yes," Vittoria replied, then added with a hint of mischief, "though your brother seemed quite concerned about their proximity to his own chambers."

Eustace nearly choked on his coffee. The minx was teasing him.

"Purely practical considerations," he said smoothly, meeting her challenging gaze across the table. "We wouldn't want to give the gossips any reason to doubt our... reconciliation."

"Of course not," she murmured, but there was something in her tone that made his blood heat. "Everything about this arrangement is purely practical, isn't it, Your Grace?"

The way she said his title—part deference, part challenge—made him want to show her just how impractical he could be.

But that way lay madness. This was a temporary solution to silence the ton's gossip, nothing more. Even if this version of his former fiancée intrigued him far more than the original ever had.

He forced his attention to his plate, but remained acutely aware of her every movement—the delicate way she buttered her toast, the graceful arch of her neck as she sipped her tea, the subtle floral scent that teased him even from across the table.

Practical indeed. If this was practicality, he was in serious trouble.

***

The afternoon light filtering through White's tall windows did nothing to improve Eustace's mood. He'd retreated to his club seeking refuge from the increasingly overwhelming presence of his supposed fiancée, only to find himself unable to focus on anything but thoughts of her.

"Ravencroft." Lord Edmund's voice cut through his brooding like a blade through silk. "Interesting choice of reading material."

Eustace glanced down at his newspaper, realizing he'd been staring at the same page for the better part of an hour. "Blackthorne," he acknowledged coldly, not bothering to rise. "To what do I owe the displeasure?"

Edmund settled uninvited into the opposite chair, his expression caught between smugness and concern. "Tell me, how is your dear countess finding London? Though perhaps I should ask how your seamstress is enjoying playing at being nobility?"

Eustace's fingers tightened on the paper, but his voice remained perfectly controlled. "I suggest you choose your next words with extreme care."

"Oh, come now." Edmund leaned forward, lowering his voice. "Surely you've noticed? The way she notices worn seams, her familiar way with servants, her complete lack of Vittoria's distinctive Italian accent?" He pulled a folded paper from his coat. "I have here testimony from three different shopkeepers in—"

Eustace's hand shot out, crumpling the paper before Edmund could finish. "If you dare breathe a word against my fiancée's reputation—"

"Your fiancée?" Edmund's eyebrows rose. "How interesting that you defend her so passionately when just this morning, my man saw her slipping into a modiste's shop through the back entrance. Rather odd behavior for a countess, wouldn't you say?"

The image rose unbidden in Eustace's mind—Vittoria's knowing comments about fabrics, her careful attention to every torn seam and loose thread in his household.

He shoved the thought aside. "I won't warn you again, Blackthorne. Leave. Her. Be."

"You're a smart man, Ravencroft. You must see the truth. That woman is no more the Countess Vittoria than I am the King of England." Edmund's voice hardened. "When this deception comes to light—and it will—your reputation will suffer alongside hers. Is that what you want? To be known as the duke who was fooled by a common—"

Eustace moved before he could think, his chair scraping back as he rose to his full height. The entire club fell silent, watching. "Choose. Your. Words. Carefully."

Something in his expression must have conveyed the depth of his rage, because Edmund paled slightly. "I merely thought, as a friend—"

"We are not friends." Eustace's voice could have frozen the Thames. "And if I hear you've been investigating my fiancée again, our next conversation will be considerably less civilized."

He strode from the club, his mind churning. The worst part wasn't Edmund's accusations—it was how they aligned with his own observations, the little details that had been nagging at him since that first night.

His carriage returned him home earlier than usual, the house quiet in the lull between afternoon calls and dinner preparations. He was heading to his study when voices from the housekeeper's sitting room caught his attention.

"—just need to reinforce the seam here," Vittoria was saying, her voice warm and confident in a way it never was in company. "See how the tension pulls at this point? If you add a line of tiny stitches..."

Eustace found himself moving closer, drawn by the natural authority in her tone.

"I never would have thought of that, miss," Mrs. Hopkins replied, sounding impressed. "Though I suppose you would know all about—"

"About the latest French techniques," Vittoria cut in quickly. "One picks up so much, traveling abroad."

Eustace peered through the partially open door. Vittoria sat with his housekeeper, her head bent over what appeared to be a torn curtain. Her fingers moved with practiced efficiency, demonstrating some sort of stitch. Gone was any trace of aristocratic aloofness—this was a woman completely in her element.

Then she laughed at something Mrs. Hopkins said, a rich, genuine sound that stirred something dangerous in his chest. He'd never heard

Vittoria laugh like that—her careful chuckle had always been measured, practiced, perfect.

Nothing about this woman was measured or practiced. Even now, she glowed with an inner fire that drew him like a moth to flame. She'd rolled her sleeves up to work, revealing delicate wrists and forearms that made his mouth go dry. A lock of hair had escaped its pins, curling against her neck in a way that made his fingers itch to brush it back.

"There," she said, holding up the curtain. "That should hold much better now. Though really, these could stand to be replaced entirely. The silk is showing wear at every seam."

"Begging your pardon, my lady, but how did you learn so much about household management?" Mrs. Hopkins asked. "I thought Italian nobles..."

Vittoria's hands stilled. "One never knows when such knowledge might be useful," she said carefully. "Even for a countess."

Eustace withdrew before they could notice him, his mind racing. Every interaction with her only deepened the mystery. If she wasn't Vittoria—and the evidence was mounting that she wasn't—then who was she? And why did the thought of her deception pain him less than the idea of losing her?

He reached his library and poured himself a generous glass of brandy, but it did nothing to calm his thoughts. The woman currently residing in his east wing was either the most changed person he'd ever encountered, or she was perpetrating an elaborate deception.

Either way, he was beginning to fear he was falling in love with her.

"Goodness," he muttered, downing the brandy in one swallow. When had his perfectly practical plan become so hopelessly complicated?

A soft knock at his study door made him stiffen. "Enter," he called, already knowing who it would be. Only one person in his household knocked quite like that.

Vittoria stepped in, still wearing her simply cut afternoon dress, that errant curl still teasing her neck. "Your Grace, I wondered if I might trouble you about the household accounts? There are some discrepancies in the—" She stopped, noticing his expression. "Is everything all right?"

No, everything was not all right. Nothing had been right since she'd walked into his life with her mysterious smiles and impossible knowledge and that laugh that haunted his dreams.

But as he looked at her, concern written across her beautiful features, he couldn't bring himself to voice his doubts. Not yet. Not until he was certain.

"Perfectly all right," he lied smoothly, gesturing to the chair across from his desk. "Now, what's this about discrepancies?"

The library had grown dim as evening approached, but Eustace couldn't bring himself to call for more candles. The fading light cast Vittoria in soft shadows as she bent over his ledgers, her finger tracing down columns of numbers with practiced ease. The intimacy of the moment felt too fragile to disturb.

"Your steward has been overcharging for grain," she murmured, so focused on the numbers that she'd forgotten to maintain her aristocratic pose. She'd drawn closer to him over the past hour, their heads nearly touching as they pored over the books together. "See this pattern here? The market prices don't match these entries."

Eustace found himself watching her lips move as she explained rather than following her calculations. This close, he could see the tiny freckle just below her left ear, smell the lavender that seemed to cling to her skin, notice how her lashes cast delicate shadows on her cheeks when she looked down.

"Your Grace?" she prompted, turning to face him. Their faces were inches apart now. "Are you listening?"

"Eustace," he said, his voice rougher than he intended. "After all, we are engaged."

A flush crept up her neck. "Eustace," she whispered, testing the name on her tongue. The sound of it sent heat coursing through his veins.

He watched, transfixed, as she unconsciously wet her lips. "The grain prices," she tried again, but her voice had lost its businesslike tone.

"Hang the grain prices," he murmured. Her breath caught as he reached up to finally, finally touch that wayward curl that had been tormenting him all evening.

His fingers brushed against the warm silk of her neck as he tucked it back, and he felt her shiver.

"W-we shouldn't," she breathed, but she didn't pull away. If anything, she swayed closer, until he could feel the warmth radiating from her body.

"Give me one good reason why not." His hand was still at her neck, his thumb tracing small circles against her pulse point. Her heartbeat raced beneath his touch.

"Because..." She seemed to struggle for words as his other hand found her waist. "Because this isn't... we agreed this was just for appearance's sake."

"Did we?" He drew her infinitesimally closer. "Strange, I'm finding it increasingly difficult to remember why I ever suggested such a foolish arrangement."

Her hands had somehow found their way to his chest, whether to push him away or pull him closer, he wasn't sure. "You said you wouldn't fall in love," she reminded him, her voice barely a whisper.

"I'm beginning to think," he said, tilting her chin up with gentle fingers, "that I may have been lying to myself."

Her eyes widened at that, something like panic flashing through them. But before he could analyze it, she surged up on her toes, eliminating all but a breath of space between their lips.

Time seemed to stop. He could feel the slight tremor in her body, see the golden flecks in her dark eyes, count every rapid breath that mingled with his own. His hand slid from her chin to cup her cheek, angling her face up as he slowly, deliberately closed that final distance—

A sharp knock shattered the moment. They sprang apart as his butler's voice called through the door: "Your Grace? Lord Zack has arrived and insists on speaking with you immediately."

Eustace murmured angrily under his breath, his hands clenching at his sides to keep from reaching for her again. Clara had retreated to the window, her chest rising and falling rapidly, her usually pristine hair charmingly mussed from his fingers.

"Tell him I'm not at home," Eustace called back, his eyes never leaving Vittoria.

"He says it's a matter of utmost urgency regarding... the new business."

"I should go," she whispered, smoothing her skirts with trembling hands. "You should speak with him."

"Stay," he said, the word somewhere between a command and a plea. "Whatever he has to say can wait."

She shook her head, already moving toward the door. "No, it can't. But..." She paused with her hand on the knob, not quite looking at him. "Thank you, Eustace."

"For what?"

"For making me wish, just for a moment, that I could be who you want me to be."

Before he could process that cryptic statement, she was gone, leaving him alone with the ledgers, the lingering scent of lavender, and the maddening memory of how perfectly she had fit in his arms.

He touched his lips, still tingling from their almost-kiss, and made a decision. Tomorrow, he would begin his own investigation into the mysterious woman who had upended his carefully ordered world. But tonight... Tonight he would allow himself to remember how close he'd come to tasting her smile.

"Goodness," he muttered for the second time that day. He was in far deeper trouble than he'd thought.

# Chapter Seven

Clara couldn't stop thinking about that almost-kiss.

She'd spent the entire morning trying to banish the memory of how close Eustace had been, how his breath had ghosted across her lips, how her heart had nearly burst from her chest—but apparently, her mind had other plans.

*Stop it,* she scolded herself for the hundredth time as she wandered the east wing corridor. *You're supposed to be a sophisticated countess, not some swooning girl.*

But every time she closed her eyes, there he was—that infuriating man with his knowing smirk and those eyes that seemed to see right through her careful facade.

"My lady?" A maid's voice snapped Clara from her thoughts. "I didn't mean to disturb you."

Clara turned to find young Betty struggling with an armful of heavy curtains, a torn section dragging on the floor. Without thinking, she reached out to help.

"Oh, careful there—you'll catch the embroidery on the—" Clara stopped herself mid-sentence, horror dawning as she realized what she was doing.

Countesses didn't notice embroidery details. They certainly didn't know how delicate silk damask could be when improperly handled.

Betty stared at her with wide eyes.

"I mean," Clara scrambled to recover, "those curtains look quite... expensive."

"They are, my lady." Betty's arms trembled under the weight. "And I've gone and torn one. Mrs. Hughes will have my head."

Clara's fingers itched to help. She knew exactly how to fix that tear—a few careful stitches with silk thread would make it invisible.

But she couldn't. She absolutely couldn't.

*Walk away,* she told herself. *That's what a countess would do.*

But Betty looked so worried, and Clara remembered all too well what it felt like to face punishment over a simple mistake.

"Here," Clara said, quickly glancing down the corridor. "Let me just—"

She'd barely taken the curtain when a familiar voice froze her in place.

"Vittoria?"

Clara's heart stopped. She turned slowly to find Eustace watching her, one eyebrow raised in that particular way that made her want to either slap him or...

*No.* She wasn't going to think about the other option.

"I was just..." She gestured vaguely at the curtains, her mind racing for an explanation that wouldn't sound completely ridiculous.

"Inspecting the furnishings?" His tone was light, but his eyes were sharp.

"Precisely." Clara lifted her chin, trying to channel every ounce of aristocratic hauteur she could muster. "One must maintain standards."

His lips twitched. "Of course."

Betty took advantage of their exchange to disappear with the curtains, leaving Clara alone with Eustace and her thundering heart.

"You seem to take quite an interest in household matters," he said, moving closer.

Too close. Close enough that she could smell him and see the faint stubble along his jaw. Close enough to remind her of that almost-kiss that definitely hadn't been haunting her thoughts.

"Well," she managed, taking a step back, "a lady should know her domain."

"Indeed." He studied her face for a long moment. "You're full of surprises, aren't you?"

Clara forced a laugh she didn't feel. "You have no idea."

She needed to escape before she did something truly stupid—like reach up and smooth that wayward lock of hair that had fallen across his forehead. Or worse, tell him the truth.

"If you'll excuse me," she said, already backing away, "I have... letters to write."

She fled before he could respond, her composure cracking with every step. This was impossible. All of it. Pretending to be someone she wasn't, living in this grand house, being near him every day...

*Get it together*, she told herself as she shut her bedroom door. *You're here to save your reputation, not lose your heart to a duke who thinks love is beneath him.*

But as she pressed her forehead against the cool wood, Clara had to admit the terrible truth—she was already falling, and there wasn't a single sewing skill in her arsenal that could stitch her heart back together when this was all over.

Eustace. That man.

"Arrogant, self-satisfied, impossible," she muttered under her breath, clenching her fists.

He hadn't even acted surprised or suspicious when he'd caught her earlier. That made it worse.

The quiet amusement in his tone, the way he looked at her—as if he saw through her and found it entertaining.

And yet, she couldn't stop thinking about him.

Clara groaned, throwing herself into the armchair by the fireplace.

This was ridiculous. She'd agreed to this sham of an engagement to protect her future, not to fall under the spell of a man who didn't believe in love.

Her gaze drifted to the mirror across the room, where her reflection stared back, frowning. "You're better than this, Clara," she said firmly, pointing at herself. "Don't let him get to you."

But it was easier said than done.

Because for every moment of his insufferable arrogance, there was another that lingered—a brief smile, a soft glance, the way his voice warmed when he spoke to his sister. She hated how her mind cataloged these little details, as if hoarding them for safekeeping.

And the almost-kiss...

Clara pressed her hands to her cheeks, trying to will away the heat rising there. That moment by the fireplace had been maddening. She could still feel the tension between them, the way his gaze had dropped to her lips like he was drawn to her against his will.

But he hadn't kissed her. He'd stopped.

"Which is a good thing," she told herself, her voice sharp in the empty room. "You don't want him to kiss you."

Except that wasn't entirely true, was it?

The thought sent a jolt through her, and she shot out of the chair, moving to the window for air. She threw it open and leaned against the frame, letting the crisp breeze cool her heated skin.

Why did he have to be so infuriatingly complex? It would've been easier if he were truly heartless. But no, Eustace had to have layers—hidden depths she couldn't stop herself from wanting to explore.

"You're losing focus," she whispered, gripping the windowsill.

She needed to remember who he was: a duke with a plan. He didn't care about her beyond what she could do for him. And she didn't care about him, not in the way that mattered. She couldn't afford to.

And yet...

Her chest tightened as memories of his rare kindnesses surfaced unbidden. His quiet defense of her during their public outings, his subtle reassurances when she faltered under society's scrutiny, and the surprising softness in his voice when he'd told her, "We do this together."

Clara turned from the window, pacing again. This wasn't supposed to happen. She wasn't supposed to feel anything for him, not admiration, not affection, and certainly not...

She pressed her hands to her face, groaning. "Stop it."

Falling for Eustace would only complicate everything. She needed to stay focused on her goal: surviving these six weeks and escaping with her secrets intact.

But as she sank back into the chair, a thought nagged at her, quiet but insistent.

What if, despite her best efforts, it was already too late?

\*\*\*

Hours later that night, Clara stared at the gown laid out on her bed, her fingers tracing the delicate beadwork she would have normally spent hours admiring. Tonight, she couldn't focus on a single stitch.

"This is ridiculous," she muttered, yanking her hands away from the fabric. "You're supposed to be preparing for a ball, not mooning over a man who explicitly said he doesn't want love."

But preparing for the ball meant spending hours getting ready to pretend to be someone she wasn't—while standing next to the very person who made her want to be herself.

Clara paced the length of her room, her stockinged feet silent on the expensive carpets. She'd dressed countless women for countless balls. She knew exactly how this was supposed to go—hair, cosmetics, gown, jewels. A perfectly orchestrated transformation into someone society deemed worthy.

Except she'd never had to do it while her heart was trying to escape her chest.

"Focus on the practical," she told herself, forcing her feet to stop moving. "You know how to do this. You've helped other women do this hundreds of times."

But none of those women had been pretending to be Italian countesses. None of them had been one wrong word away from complete ruin. And none of them had been falling for a duke who thought love was a waste of time.

Clara grabbed her hairbrush with more force than necessary, attacking her curls as if they were responsible for her current predicament.

"Ouch!" She glared at her reflection. "This is exactly what you get for being foolish enough to—"

A knock at the door nearly sent her jumping out of her skin.

"My lady?" It was Martha, one of the maids. "His Grace asked me to assist you with dressing."

Clara's heart did that ridiculous fluttering thing again. Even his thoughtfulness was infuriating.

"Come in, Martha."

The maid entered with an array of cosmetics and hair pins, and Clara had to stop herself from automatically reaching for them herself. She wasn't the one who helped others prepare anymore. She was the one being helped.

As Martha worked, Clara closed her eyes, trying to imagine herself as the confident countess she was supposed to be.

Instead, all she could see was Eustace's face when he'd caught her with the curtains. That knowing look in his eyes, like he could see straight through every lie she'd told.

She hoped she was wrong. Maybe it was just paranoia.

"You look beautiful, my lady."

Clara opened her eyes to find Martha beaming at her handiwork. The woman in the mirror looked exactly like what she was supposed to be—elegant, refined, every inch a countess.

So why did she feel more like an imposter than ever?

She stood, letting Martha help her into the evening gown—midnight blue silk that would have made her professional fingers itch to examine the construction, if she weren't so distracted by the knowledge that she'd soon be dancing in Eustace's arms while wearing it.

"Stop it," she whispered to herself.

"My lady?"

"Nothing." Clara forced a smile. "Thank you, Martha. You've done wonders."

The maid curtsied and left, leaving Clara alone with her reflection and her treacherous thoughts.

She grabbed her fan, practicing the sharp snap that usually made her feel powerful. Tonight it just felt like another prop in this elaborate charade.

"You can do this," she told her reflection. "Just a few more weeks. Don't feel anything. Don't want anything. And definitely don't think about how his hands feel when you're dancing, or how his eyes crinkle at the corners when he's trying not to smile, or how—"

Another knock, harder this time.

"Vittoria?" Eustace's voice sent her pulse racing. "The carriage is ready."

Clara took one last look in the mirror, straightening her shoulders and lifting her chin. She could do this. She had to do this.

But as she opened the door to find Eustace waiting, devastatingly handsome in his evening clothes, she knew she was lying to herself.

She was already in far too deep, and tonight was only going to make it worse.

The ballroom of Berkeley House sparkled like something from a dream, all gilt and crystal and candlelight. Clara might have appreciated its grandeur more if she weren't so focused on not tripping over her own feet—or her words.

"You're unusually quiet tonight," Eustace murmured as they moved through the crowd. His hand at the small of her back felt like it was burning through her gown.

"I'm being mysterious and alluring."

"Is that what this is?"

She shot him a look that would have been more effective if her heart wasn't trying to escape through her throat. "Would you prefer I cause a scene? I could swoon dramatically into the punch bowl."

His lips twitched. "Save that for after the first dance, at least."

Music filled the air—the opening strains of a waltz.

Eustace was beside her, his hand resting lightly on her arm as they navigated the crowd. His touch burned through the layers of her gown, steadying her even as it made her pulse race. He was playing his part perfectly—the attentive fiancé, the picture of propriety.

If only she could say the same for herself.

Clara forced her focus back to her surroundings, scanning the room.

Lord Edmund was here somewhere; she could feel his presence like a storm cloud looming on the horizon. The man had been spreading all kinds of rumors about her that she really feared meeting.

She had avoided him all evening, weaving through the crowd with carefully planned precision. But each moment of reprieve felt borrowed, the inevitable confrontation ticking closer.

She stiffened as Eustace leaned down, his voice low and close to her ear. "Relax, Vittoria. You look like you're bracing for battle."

Her lips curved into a sharp smile. "Perhaps I am."

His chuckle was soft, meant only for her, and it sent a shiver down her spine. "No one's going to find fault with you tonight," he said, his gaze sweeping the room. "They wouldn't dare. You're with me."

The confidence in his voice both comforted and infuriated her. "Oh, well then," she said lightly, "I suppose I'll just leave my worries at the door."

"Good idea," he replied, his lips quirking in amusement.

They made their way to the dance floor, and as the music shifted to a slower waltz, Eustace turned to her. "Shall we?"

Clara hesitated, but his outstretched hand left her little choice. She placed her gloved fingers in his, allowing him to guide her onto the polished floor.

The first few steps were careful, measured. Clara focused on keeping her movements graceful, on not tripping over her own feet. But as the music swelled and Eustace's hand pressed gently against the small of her back, the tension began to ebb.

"You're still being mysterious," he said as they turned.

"And you're still talking."

They moved together perfectly, as if they'd been dancing for years instead of weeks.

She caught a glimpse of Lord Edmund watching from the edge of the ballroom and missed a step.

Eustace's arm tightened around her waist. "Careful."

"Sorry, I—" She forced her eyes away from Edmund's predatory gaze. "The floor must be slippery."

"Must be." But his tone said he didn't believe her for a second.

She risked a glance up at him. His face was unreadable, but his touch was firm, his movements steady as he guided her through the dance. For a moment, she let herself forget the lies, the secrets, the watching eyes.

For a moment, it was just them.

"You're getting better at this," he murmured, his voice so low it sent a ripple through her.

"At pretending?" she asked, unable to keep the bitterness from her tone.

"At dancing," he said, his lips twitching with the ghost of a smile.

Clara's heart betrayed her, skipping a beat. She looked away, focusing on the sea of swirling gowns around them.

But when his hand tightened slightly on her waist, her resolve wavered. The way he looked at her, the warmth in his eyes—it all felt too real.

This wasn't supposed to happen. She wasn't supposed to feel this way, to want to close the distance between them, to forget for just a moment…

The music swelled, the final note hanging in the air as Eustace guided her into a spin. When they stopped, her breath was stolen, her chest tight with emotions she couldn't name.

The applause broke the spell, and Clara stepped back, her mask slipping for just a moment. She glanced up at him, her lips parting to speak—

"Clara Mills!"

The voice cut through the crowd like a blade, freezing her in place.

The room fell silent. Clara turned slowly, her heart sinking as Lord Edmund stepped forward, his expression triumphant.

"Mills," he repeated, his voice dripping with venom. "Not Vittoria Romano. Not a countess. A seamstress, a fraud."

Clara's breath caught in her throat. The faces surrounding her blurred into a sea of shock and judgment. She took a step back, her pulse hammering in her ears.

"This woman," Edmund continued, addressing the crowd, "is no aristocrat. She is an imposter, a common seamstress pretending to be someone she's not."

"No," Clara whispered, but her voice was drowned out by the murmurs rising around her.

Clara felt the blood drain from her face, Eustace's hand tightened on hers, but she barely felt it through the roaring in her ears.

Eustace moved, his presence suddenly between her and Edmund. His voice, calm and deliberate, silenced the room. "That's enough."

Edmund sneered. "Oh, come now, Eustace. Surely you don't believe this charade. Or have you been taken in as well?"

Eustace's gaze was ice. "I believe in my fiancée. And I have proof to silence your slander."

Clara's blood turned cold. Proof? What was he talking about?

Eustace turned slightly, his hand reaching for hers. "You all remember Vittoria's distinctive birthmark," he said, his voice steady. "Shall I show you?"

Clara's heart stopped. The birthmark. The one she didn't have.

She tried to pull back, but Eustace's grip on her hand tightened, his gaze locking onto hers.

"Don't," she whispered, her voice trembling.

His expression softened, just for a moment, but his grip didn't loosen. "Trust me," he murmured.

But Clara couldn't.

Not when everything she'd worked for was hanging by a thread. She wrenched her hand free, stepping back.

The crowd gasped, the tension in the room reaching its peak. Edmund's smirk widened, and Clara's panic surged.

Her voice shook as she took another step back. "Please... don't do this."

But it was too late. The truth—or a version of it—was about to unravel. And Clara wasn't sure she could survive what came next.

# Chapter Eight

The ballroom at Berkeley House blazed with a hundred candles, but Eustace felt the heat of Vittoria's hand against his arm more keenly than any flame. Edmund's accusation still rang through the shocked silence.

Time seemed to slow as Eustace acted on instinct, his larger hand engulfing Vittoria's delicate one. He felt her pulse jump wildly beneath his fingers as he turned her hand over, his thumb brushing across her inner wrist in a caress that was far more intimate than the moment called for.

She begged, eyes wide and filled with unshed tears and it almost made him pause.

But he had to do this.

Why was she so afraid?

"My fiancée," he announced to the breathlessly waiting crowd, his voice carrying that ducal authority that brooked no argument, "bears a rather distinctive birthmark. One that I remember quite well from our childhood."

Vittoria's sharp intake of breath was audible only to him as he pushed back the lace at her wrist. The motion made her sway slightly toward him, and the subtle scent of lavender and warm skin nearly derailed his thoughts entirely.

"Perhaps," he continued, fighting to keep his voice steady as his fingers traced dangerous patterns against her sensitive skin, "Lord Edmund would care to explain how a common seamstress came to possess the exact same mark as the Countess Vittoria Romano?"

There it was – a small, crescent-shaped mark on her pinky finger. Exactly where it should be. Exactly as he remembered.

The triumph of silencing Edmund warred with the surge of suspicion that rose in his chest. But those thoughts scattered when Vittoria's fingers curled involuntarily against his palm, her short nails scraping lightly across his skin.

Heat bloomed between them, inappropriate for the public setting but impossible to ignore. When he dared to look down at her, the mixture of fear, gratitude, and something darker in her eyes made his blood sing.

"Well?" he demanded of Edmund, though it took considerable effort to drag his attention away from the woman trembling slightly against him. "Do you have anything else to add to your ridiculous accusations?"

Edmund's face had gone an interesting shade of puce. "I... that is to say..."

"No?" Eustace raised an eyebrow, his thumb still drawing maddening circles on Vittoria's wrist. "Then I suggest you take your leave before you embarrass yourself further."

The crowd parted like the Red Sea as Edmund stormed out. Whispers erupted in his wake, but Eustace barely heard them. He was too focused on the way Vittoria was looking at him—equal parts relief and something that looked dangerously like desire.

"A dance, I think," he said softly, pulling her closer than strictly necessary. "To show these vultures that their gossip hasn't affected us."

Her eyes widened. "Eustace, I—"

"Hush," he murmured, leading her to the dance floor as the opening strains of a waltz began. "Let them see exactly what I see when I look at you."

"And what is that?" she whispered as he pulled her into his arms, one hand spanning her waist while the other still held hers captive.

Instead of answering, he drew her closer than propriety allowed, feeling the soft curves of her body align with his. She fit against him perfectly—too perfectly. Nothing about her was what he expected, what he remembered of Vittoria, and yet...

"You," he said finally, his lips brushing her ear as they moved together, "are the most maddening contradiction I have ever encountered."

Her breath hitched. "I don't know what you mean."

"Don't you?" He tightened his grip infinitesimally on her waist, feeling her shiver. "Why were you afraid? You are the countess, the birthmark showed it, it's been there since the day you were born."

"Oh." She whispered, then gasped as he executed a turn that pressed her even more firmly against him.

"If I knew for sure you were Vittoria." His thumb stroked over it again, a silent warning or a caress—he wasn't quite sure himself anymore. "Why did you beg me?"

Their eyes met, and the heat in her gaze nearly undid him. She was lying to him—he was almost certain of it now. But God help him, he was starting to think he didn't care.

"Eustace," she breathed, and his name on her lips was both a prayer and a sin.

He leaned down until his lips nearly brushed hers, propriety ignored. "Who are you really?" he whispered against her mouth.

But the music ended before she could answer, leaving them both breathing hard and aching for more than answers.

Two days after the ball, Eustace found himself doing something entirely beneath his dignity as a duke—lurking in the shadows of London's merchant district, following his supposed betrothed.

The early morning fog provided convenient cover as he watched Vittoria slip into yet another seamstress's shop, her figure disguised by a plain brown cloak.

This was the third such establishment she'd visited. At each one, she carried herself with the easy familiarity of someone who belonged in these working-class environs. Not at all like a countess who should be taking tea in Mayfair.

"Just a few adjustments to the bodice, Mrs. Harrison," Vittoria's voice drifted through the shop's open window. "And perhaps we could let out the seams here? Your daughter will grow quickly at her age."

"Bless you, miss. We couldn't afford—"

"Nonsense. Growing girls need proper dresses. Consider it done."

Eustace found himself moving closer, drawn by the warmth in her voice. Through the window, he caught glimpses of her working—quick, confident movements of her hands as she pinned fabric, the gentle way she guided a young apprentice's stitches. She looked more at ease here than she ever had at his dinner table.

His chest tightened with an unfamiliar ache. This woman—whoever she truly was—possessed a kindness that couldn't be feigned. It showed in every interaction, from the way she spoke to merchants' wives as equals to how she slipped extra coins to street children when she thought no one was watching.

By midday, he'd watched her provide free mending to an elderly widow, offer employment to a desperate young mother, and haggle with a fabric merchant on behalf of a struggling dressmaker. Each act of kindness felt like another twist of the knife in his chest. How could someone capable of such genuine compassion be engaged in a grand deception?

*Unless*, a treacherous voice whispered in his mind, *she has good reason for her secrets.*

\*\*\*

"The girl is not who she claims to be, Eustace."

His mother's voice, usually so gentle, carried an edge of steel as she confronted him in his study that evening.

The Dowager Duchess of Ravencroft was not a woman easily fooled, and her pale blue eyes fixed him with an unwavering stare.

"I assume you have evidence for such an accusation?" Eustace kept his tone carefully neutral as he poured them both a glass of sherry. The crystal decanter clinked against the glasses with more force than necessary.

"Evidence? I have eyes, son." She accepted the glass but didn't drink. "The way she moves, her manner of speech, her knowledge of household matters—she is not the shy, scholarly girl I remember from Italy."

"People change, Mother. It's been years."

"Not that much." She set down her untouched sherry. "I watched her yesterday, instructing the maids on removing wine stains from silk. Since when does a countess know such things?"

Eustace turned to the window, watching the late afternoon shadows lengthen across his gardens. Somewhere in the east wing, Vittoria would be preparing for dinner, perhaps humming those working-class ballads she thought no one heard.

"Perhaps," he said slowly, "you should consider that any changes in her are improvements. The Vittoria you knew could hardly maintain a conversation. This one—" He caught himself smiling. "This one challenges me at every turn."

"And that pleases you?" His mother's voice softened with surprise.

"More than it should." The admission cost him, but there it was. "Whatever secrets she carries, whatever game she plays—she has made these past weeks the most engaging of my life."

"You're falling in love with her."

It wasn't a question. Eustace didn't answer, but his silence was confirmation enough.

"Just be careful, my darling boy," his mother sighed, rising to leave. "A woman with secrets has reasons for them. And those reasons may break more than just your pride."

"I know exactly what I'm doing, Mother."

But as he stood alone in his study, watching the sun set over London, Eustace wondered if that was the biggest lie of all.

Later that night, when the rest of the household slept, he caught the whisper of silk against wood—Vittoria, sneaking through the corridors again. Instead of following, he waited in his study, pouring two glasses of brandy. She would walk past eventually. She always did.

When her shadow darkened his doorway, he spoke without looking up. "Either you're taking midnight walks to improve your health, or you're looking for something in my house. Which is it?"

He heard her sharp intake of breath, then the soft rustle of her dressing gown as she stepped into the lamplight. "Perhaps I simply find it difficult to sleep in strange houses."

"You've been here three weeks." Finally, he turned to face her. "It's hardly strange anymore."

In the low light, with her hair falling loose around her shoulders and her eyes bright with wariness, she looked both more and less like Vittoria than ever. The real countess would never have dared to wander a gentleman's house at night. Yet somehow, she made it seem natural, as though she belonged in these shadowed halls as much as she belonged in his thoughts.

"Who are you?" he asked softly. "Really?"

She lifted her chin, defiant even in her vulnerability. "I am exactly who you need me to be, Your Grace."

"That's not an answer."

"No," she agreed, taking the brandy he offered. "But it's all I can give you tonight."

Their fingers brushed during the exchange, and Eustace fought the urge to capture her hand, to demand real answers. Instead, he watched as she sipped the brandy with the same elegant poise she showed at dinner parties. Another contradiction. Another mystery.

"Goodnight, Your Grace," she murmured, setting down the glass. But she hesitated in the doorway, looking back at him with an expression that made his heart stutter. "Thank you for today. At the shops."

Before he could respond, she was gone, leaving only the lingering scent of lavender and the echo of her words. She had known he was following her. Of course she had.

Eustace downed his brandy in one burning swallow. He was trapped in a web of secrets and lies, and God help him, he was starting to prefer it to any truth that might take her away from him.

\*\*\*

## TWO DAYS LATER

The midnight hour had long passed when Eustace finally set aside the estate ledgers. His eyes burned from squinting at columns of numbers, but his mind was too restless for sleep. Every time he closed his eyes, he saw Vittoria's face in the lamplight two days ago, heard the quiet challenge in her voice: *I am exactly who you need me to be.*

A soft knock at his study door drew his attention. He knew who it was before she entered—only Vittoria would dare disturb him at this hour. She had developed an uncanny habit of appearing just when his thoughts turned to her, as if she could sense his internal turmoil.

"Your Grace?" She stepped into the room, still fully dressed despite the late hour. The dark blue of her gown made her skin seem to glow in the candlelight. "I saw the light under your door."

"Did you come to confess?" The words slipped out before he could stop them, rough with brandy and frustration. "Or to spin more pretty lies?"

Vittoria's steps faltered, but she didn't retreat. Instead, she moved closer, until she stood on the opposite side of his desk. "I came because you looked troubled at dinner. But perhaps I was mistaken in thinking you might want company."

Eustace stood, unable to maintain the pretense of working while she stood there, somehow making his massive study feel impossibly small. "Troubled?" He gave a harsh laugh. "Yes, I suppose a man might be troubled when he finds himself harboring a woman who refuses to tell him who she truly is."

"You know who I am." But her fingers twisted in her skirts, betraying her nervousness. "You've known me since we were children. And now what? Do you also believe I'm not Vittoria?"

"Do I?" He rounded the desk, watching as she held her ground. "I know you have Vittoria's face. Her birthmark. Even her way of tilting her head when you're thinking." He reached out, his fingers hovering near her cheek but not quite touching. "But that was the Vittoria I knew as a very young child. You still look like the Vittoria I got betrothed to, but that Vittoria? She was nothing like her childhood self and you. You only have her face, everything else—your wit, your passion, the way you light up a room instead of hiding in corners—that is very different."

A flush crept up her neck, but her gaze remained steady. "Perhaps you never really knew Vittoria at all."

"No games," he growled, finally giving in to the urge to touch her, his hand cupping her cheek. "No more clever deflections. I watched you today, moving through those shops like you belonged there. I've seen the calluses on your fingers that no countess would have. I've noticed how you know things about household management that Vittoria never cared to learn."

Vittoria didn't pull away from his touch, but he felt her tremble. "You've not cared about me in five years? And you think you know anything about me?"

He keeps quiet, his thumb traced the curve of her cheekbone, feeling the warmth of her blush. "You are right."

"Am I?"

"You are." He stepped closer, close enough to catch the faint scent of lavender that always clung to her skin. "I'm sorry, Vittoria. I know it is you, it's just hard reconciling the image of you in my head with what I see before me. It's hard thinking about the fact that I broke off our engagement because I thought you... you weren't what I wanted. But now... now I find myself following you through London just to watch you smile at shopkeepers' children. Now I realize I look forward to our arguments more than I've ever looked forward to anything. Now

I catch myself wondering if your hair would feel as soft as it looks, if your lips would taste like—"

"Don't." She pressed her fingers to his lips, stopping the words. "Please don't say things you'll regret later."

Eustace caught her wrist, holding her hand in place. "I won't regret it later."

"I am a woman who cannot give you what you want," she whispered. "And you are a man who deserves more."

Before he could stop her, she turned and fled the study, leaving him alone with the ghost of her touch on his skin and the bitter taste of unspoken truths in his mouth.

Eustace sank into his chair, running a hand over his face. He should end this. He should end this before he lands himself where he can't come out of. Instead, he found himself remembering the way she'd looked at him, the mix of longing and fear in her eyes.

"Blast it all to hell," he muttered, reaching for the brandy decanter.

# Chapter Nine

Clara stood before her mirror, adjusting her bonnet for the third time that morning.

The pale blue silk caught the light, its soft sheen making her think of morning skies after a rain.

Feathers curved delicately along one side, whispering elegance without shouting it. The ribbons, wide and satin-smooth, framed her face before tying into an impeccable bow beneath her chin.

She reached up, tugging a little at the brim, ensuring the lace lining peeked out just enough to soften the edges. It was absurd, really—how something as simple as a bonnet could wield so much power.

Wear it the wrong way, and you looked like a girl trying too hard to be grand. Wear it the right way, and...

Two weeks down, four to go. Just four more weeks of pretending to be someone she wasn't, four more weeks of watching every word, every gesture, every reaction.

She could do this. She had to do this.

"You're being ridiculous," she muttered to her reflection, straightening her shoulders. "You've fooled them this long. What's another month?"

But her hands trembled as she smoothed down her morning dress, and she couldn't shake the feeling that everything was about to fall apart. Just yesterday, she'd caught Duchess Dowager studying her with that particular look—the one that said she'd noticed something off about her son's supposedly long-lost fiancée.

And then there was Eustace's sister, Margaret, with her endless questions about Italy and childhood memories Clara couldn't possibly answer. Even the servants were starting to exchange knowing glances whenever she forgot herself and showed too much knowledge of household matters.

"Focus," she whispered, pinching her cheeks for color. "You're Vittoria Romano, Countess of... somewhere. You most certainly do not know how to darn socks or the proper way to press a cravat."

The garden party awaiting her downstairs would be her first proper public outing as Eustace's "reconciled" fiancée. Every eye would be watching, every tongue ready to wag at the slightest misstep.

Clara's stomach churned. She'd dressed countless ladies for occasions like this, standing in the shadows as they'd fretted over every detail. Now she was the one who'd be scrutinized, and her entire future hung on her performance.

"You can do this," she told her reflection again, but the woman staring back looked about as convinced as she felt.

A knock at her door made her jump.

"My lady?" It was Martha, "His Grace asks if you're ready. The first guests are arriving."

Clara's heart skipped. Eustace. Even thinking his name sent a flutter through her chest that had nothing to do with anxiety and everything to do with the way he'd looked at her yesterday across the dinner table, like he could see straight through every lie she'd told.

"Coming," she called, forcing her voice to stay steady. "Just a moment."

She gave herself one last look in the mirror. The woman staring back was perfectly put together, every curl in place, every ribbon precisely tied. No one would guess that beneath all the silk and lace was a seamstress playing the greatest role of her life.

Or that she was absolutely terrified of what the next four weeks would bring.

Clara squared her shoulders and lifted her chin. Time to give the performance of her life. Again.

After all, what choice did she have?

\*\*\*

Clara's fingers tightened around her fan as she spotted a familiar silhouette across the garden.

It couldn't be. Not here.

Not today.

But there was no mistaking Thomas's hulking frame, even at this distance. Her stepbrother lingered near the garden wall, his presence as subtle as a wolf among lambs.

The late afternoon sun suddenly felt too bright, too harsh. Clara retreated beneath a flowering arbor, memories rushing back.

"Look at her, thinking she's better than us just because she can thread a needle."

Thomas's mocking voice echoed from the past, accompanied by the sharp crack of her sewing box hitting the floor. Her precious needles, scattered across dirty floorboards. Spools of thread rolling under furniture while James laughed.

She'd spent hours collecting those supplies, saving every penny...

"Are you quite well, my dear?"

Clara startled. Duchess Dowager stood before her, concern etched across her aristocratic features.

"Perfectly well." Clara forced her lips into a smile. "The sun is rather warm today."

*"Too fine to eat with us now, are you?"*

Past and present collided as she remembered that night, three years ago, when she'd missed dinner to finish a crucial commission.

Her father's rage. The locked door. Two days without food.

But she'd finished the dress. And the payment had helped establish her as Madame Celestine.

"Perhaps some lemonade?" Duchess Dowager's voice drew her back.

Clara nodded, grateful for the excuse to move deeper into the crowd of parasols and elegant day dresses. She'd survived worse than this. She'd built herself from nothing, stitch by careful stitch.

A cluster of young ladies nearby tittered behind their fans, exchanging knowing looks as she passed. Let them whisper. They had no idea what real scandal was.

*"You'll never be more than a servant,"* her father had sneered when she'd opened her shop. *"Playing at being a proper businesswoman."*

Well. Here she was now, playing at being a proper lady. The irony wasn't lost on her.

"There you are, darling."

Eustace's voice wrapped around her like silk. He appeared at her elbow, solid and reassuring, offering his arm.

Clara took it, letting his presence ground her. He might not love her—might never love her—but right now, he was her anchor in this glittering sea of potential disasters.

"I believe Lady Pembroke is asking after you," he said. "Something about that fascinating blue gown you wore at the Hartley's ball?"

If he noticed how tightly she gripped his arm, he didn't mention it. And if she noticed Thomas skulking away from the garden wall, well... she wouldn't mention that either.

She had four more weeks of this masquerade. Four weeks to untangle herself from both her past and present without destroying everything she'd built.

Clara lifted her chin and smiled brilliantly at the approaching Lady Pembroke. She could do this. She would do this.

After all, she'd already succeeded at the impossible once—a nobody who became London's most sought-after modiste.

Compared to that, surely maintaining a false identity among the ton while avoiding her blackmailing family was nothing.

Right?

The afternoon tea service arrived with its usual pageantry of silver trays and delicate porcelain. Clara had just lifted her cup when she saw it—a folded note tucked beneath her saucer, James's cramped handwriting visible through the paper.

Her hand trembled, tea sloshing dangerously close to the cup's rim.

"More sugar?"

Lady Margaret's voice dripped honey-sweet across the table. Clara forced herself to look up, to smile, to play her part. The note burned against her palm like a hot coal.

"No, thank you." Keep breathing. Keep smiling. Don't let them see. "Though these lemon cakes are divine."

"Aren't they?" Duchess Dowager beamed. "Our cook is quite talented with French pastries. You must have had far superior ones in Italy, of course."

Clara's stomach clenched. Another lie to juggle. Another thread that could unravel everything.

She waited until the conversation drifted to the latest on-dit before slipping the note open in her lap.

*We know what you are doing! Father wants to discuss terms. Tonight. The usual place. Come if you don't want us to expose you.*

The emerald necklace. Of course. She'd sold it last week to pay their first round of demands, claiming it had been lost. The gardens swam before her eyes.

"Vittoria?" Eustace's hand brushed her arm. "You've gone quite pale."

She looked up into his concerned face and felt something crack inside her chest. He'd been nothing but kind, even if it was all for show. And here she was, lying to him with every breath.

"Just a touch of heat," she managed. "Perhaps some air?"

"Allow me to escort you to the terrace."

But before they could rise, Lady Rutledge swept in with her latest protégé in tow, demanding introductions. Clara tucked the note into her sleeve, its edges sharp against her skin.

More names to remember. More lies to maintain. More pieces of herself fracturing with every perfectly practiced curtsy.

"And how did you find the opera season in Milan?" Lady Rutledge fixed her with that razor-sharp stare that had undoubtedly ruined a dozen reputations over the years.

Clara opened her mouth, ready to spin another tale, when she caught sight of Eustace watching her. Something in his expression made her breath catch.

He knew. He had to know. Right?

How could he not? And why does he keep looking at me like that?

But instead of doing anything, he smoothly intercepted Lady Rutledge's question with a story about his own travels abroad. Clara sank back in her chair, relief warring with a fresh wave of guilt.

The note crinkled in her sleeve. The tea turned to ashes in her mouth. And somewhere in the garden, her father waited to destroy everything she'd built.

Four more weeks suddenly felt like an eternity.

Through the drawing room windows, Clara caught sight of her father's signal—that same cruel, two-fingered gesture he'd used when she was a child. Her stomach lurched.

"I believe I'll take that air now," she murmured, setting down her tea with trembling hands. "Please, don't let me disturb the party."

"Shall I accompany you?" Eustace half-rose from his seat.

"No!" Too sharp. Too quick. She softened her tone. "I mean, Duchess Dowager was just asking about your travels in Venice. I won't be but a moment."

The garden's edge felt miles away from the laughter and tinkling china. Clara's slippers whispered against the gravel path as she approached the shadowy figure waiting beneath the oak tree.

Her father hadn't changed—still wearing that same smug smile that had haunted her childhood nightmares.

"Well, well. If it isn't the *countess*." He spat the title like a curse. "Quite a performance you're giving."

Clara's nails dug into her palms. "What do you want?"

"Now, is that any way to greet your dear papa?" He asked, moving closer. "Especially when I hold your entire future in my hands."

"You're not my father." The words came out sharper than she intended. Braver than she felt. "And you never were."

"No?" His smile widened. "Then perhaps I should go tell your fine duke about the little guttersnipe who's been playing dress-up in his world. Two thousand pounds might convince me to keep quiet."

The amount hit her like a physical blow. "Two thou—That's impossible! I don't have that kind of money!"

"Oh, but you do." He gestured toward the party. "Or rather, your *fiancé* does. I'm sure a woman of your... talents... can figure something out."

Blood roared in Clara's ears. Everything she'd worked for, everything she'd built, balanced on a knife's edge.

"I won't steal from him."

"Then I suppose you'll enjoy debtor's prison. I wonder what they'll do to you when they discover your deception? Fraud against the nobility—that's quite serious."

A burst of laughter from the party made her flinch. She could see Eustace through the trees, his tall frame unmistakable among the guests. What would he think when he learned the truth?

"Two days." Her stepfather's voice hardened. "That's all you get. And Vittoria?" He caught her arm as she turned to leave, using her false name like another weapon. "Try anything clever, and I'll make sure every drawing room in London knows exactly what you are."

She yanked free, nearly stumbling in her haste to escape. Her careful world was crumbling, and she couldn't stop it.

Tears burned behind her eyes as she wove through the garden. She couldn't go back to the party like this. Couldn't face their scrutiny, their questions. Couldn't bear to see Eustace's kindness when she knew she'd have to betray it.

Finding a hidden alcove, Clara pressed her forehead against cool stone and finally let herself shake. Two thousand pounds. It might as well have been the moon.

*What choice do you have?* The voice in her head sounded terrifyingly like her stepfather's. *You're nothing but a fraud. You always have been.*

"Vittoria."

She whirled to find Eustace watching her, his expression unreadable in the shadows. How long had he been there? What had he seen?

"I—" Her voice cracked. "I needed a moment."

"They're asking for you inside." His voice was gentle, concerned, making everything so much worse.

She took his offered arm, hating how much she wanted to lean into his strength. Four more weeks. She just had to survive four more weeks.

But first, she had to survive the next two days.

Clara straightened her shoulders and fixed her brightest smile in place. Time to give the performance of her life.

Again.

After all, what choice did she have?

## Chapter Ten

Eustace Montague studied the social calendar spread across his breakfast table with the same tactical precision he might apply to a military campaign.

Each event had been carefully selected, each appearance meticulously timed.

He narrowed his eyes as he remembered their last outing. Something had happened to Vittoria.

He had no idea what it was.

He took a sip of his morning coffee, black and bitter like his current mood, as he made another notation in his leather-bound notebook.

"Is plotting our social demise so entertaining, Your Grace?"

Vittoria's voice, touched with early morning huskiness, drew his attention. She stood in the doorway of his private breakfast room, already dressed in a morning gown of pale blue silk. The sight of her—fresh and lovely in the morning light—made his chest tighten in a now-familiar way.

"Plotting our success, actually," he corrected, forcing his gaze back to his papers. "The Rutherfords' garden party this afternoon, followed by Lady Ashworth's musical evening. Both events carefully chosen for their relative privacy and controlled guest lists."

"How very... militant of you." She settled into the chair opposite him, reaching for the tea service. The morning sun caught the delicate bones of her wrist as she poured, and Eustace found himself tracking the movement with unnecessary attention.

"Someone has to maintain order in this chaos you've created," he said dryly, though his lips twitched at her answering smile. "Or would you prefer I leave our public appearances to chance?"

"Heaven forbid." She doctored her tea with honey. "Though I do wonder if all these social engagements are strictly necessary."

Eustace leaned back, studying her face. There was tension around her eyes today, a slight tightness to her smile that most would miss. But he'd become an expert in reading her expressions over the past weeks, cataloging each minute change like a man obsessed.

"They are if we want society to believe in our... reconciliation." He kept his voice neutral, though the word tasted false on his tongue. "The ton must see us together, content and engaged, or rumors will start."

"More rumors, you mean." She stirred her tea absently. "Sometimes I think you enjoy this performance a bit too much, Your Grace."

If she only knew. He enjoyed it far too much—watching her charm their peers, standing close enough to catch the lavender scent of her hair, playing the role of devoted fiancée. It was becoming dangerously easy to forget it was all pretense.

\*\*\*

The Rutherfords' garden party was in full swing when Eustace first noticed them—two men in unremarkable brown coats, lingering at the edges of the gathering. Their attention seemed fixed on Vittoria as she moved through the crowd, laughing at Lady Rutherford's jokes and admiring the rose garden.

Something about their watchfulness set his teeth on edge.

"Your fiancée is quite charming," Lord Pembroke observed, joining him near the refreshment table. "Quite different from what I remember of her in Italy."

"People change," Eustace replied automatically, his eyes never leaving Vittoria. She had stopped by a fountain, and even from this distance, he could see how her fingers worried at her fan—a sure sign of distress.

A footman approached her with a silver tray. Among the glasses of lemonade lay a folded note. Vittoria's face remained perfectly composed as she took it, but Eustace saw the slight tremor in her hands as she tucked it into her reticule.

The mysterious observers shifted closer.

"If you'll excuse me," Eustace murmured to Pembroke, already moving. Within moments, he was at Vittoria's side, his hand settling possessively at the small of her back.

"Is everything all right, my dear?" He kept his voice low, meant only for her ears.

"Perfectly fine." But she leaned into his touch ever so slightly, betraying her need for support. "Though perhaps we might take a turn about the garden? The sun is rather warm."

He guided her toward a more secluded path, noting how the two men remained just within sight. "You know," he said conversationally, "most women would trust their fiancés with their troubles."

"Most women aren't fake engaged to such observant dukes." She attempted a light tone, but he felt the tension thrumming through her body where his hand still rested against her back.

"Vittoria." He stopped walking, turning her to face him. In the dappled shade of an oak tree, her eyes seemed almost green. "Whatever is wrong, whatever has you looking over your shoulder—let me help."

For a moment, something raw and vulnerable flickered across her face. She swayed toward him slightly, as if fighting the urge to seek shelter in his arms. Then her expression smoothed over, that mask of serenity sliding back into place.

"Nothing is wrong that time won't cure," she said softly. "Please, don't concern yourself."

The carriage ride home that evening was thick with unspoken words. Eustace watched Vittoria from the corner of his eye as she stared out the window, her fingers absently tracing the edge of her reticule where that mysterious note still lay hidden.

The two men in brown coats had followed their carriage for three blocks before falling behind.

"You know," he said finally, breaking the tense silence, "when I arranged this charade, I didn't expect to find myself playing protector as well as fiancé."

Vittoria's head turned sharply. "I don't need protection."

"Don't you?" He leaned forward, bracing his elbows on his knees. "Then perhaps you can explain the men who've been watching our every move? Or the note that made you pale beneath your powder? Or why you've barely slept this past week?"

"You've been watching me sleep?" A poor attempt at deflection, but he noticed she didn't deny his other observations.

"I notice everything about you," he admitted, the words rougher than intended. "Whether I want to or not."

She looked away first, her fingers clenching in the fabric of her skirts. "Some secrets are better left buried, Your Grace."

"Not if they're causing you harm."

The carriage pulled up to his townhouse before she could respond. As he helped her down, his hands lingering perhaps longer than necessary on her waist, Eustace made a silent vow. Whatever shadows were haunting Vittoria, whatever secrets she was protecting—he would uncover them.

Because the thought of her facing those shadows alone made something fierce and protective rise in his chest. Something that felt dangerously close to love.

He watched her disappear into the house, her blue skirts swishing around corners until she was gone. Then he turned to his butler, his expression grim.

"Harrison, I want every footman we can spare watching the house tonight. And send word to my investigator. It seems we have some uninvited admirers to look into."

The game had changed. And Eustace Montague had never been one to lose.

***

DAYS LATER

Eustace stood at the edge of Lady Ashworth's ballroom, his fingers tightening around his crystal glass as he watched yet another simpering fool bow over Vittoria's hand.

The third one this evening. Not that he was counting.

"Your grace." Lord Pembroke's voice drew his attention. "I couldn't help but notice your... intense observation of the crowd."

"Merely ensuring the night goes smoothly," Eustace replied, his tone clipped. But his eyes never left Vittoria as she gracefully sidestepped the young lord's obvious attempt to secure a dance.

She was magnificent tonight in a gown of deep burgundy silk. The way she moved through the crowd with such natural elegance was beautiful.

"Smooth indeed," Pembroke drawled. "Though I dare say Lord Rutherford seems quite taken with your... fiancée."

Eustace's jaw clenched. Rutherford. The boy was barely out of leading strings, yet he'd been hovering around Vittoria all evening like a moth to flame.

"If you'll excuse me." Eustace set down his glass with more force than necessary and strode across the ballroom.

He reached Vittoria just as Rutherford was attempting to lead her toward the terrace. "My dear," Eustace interrupted smoothly, though there was steel beneath his smile. "I believe you promised me this dance."

Vittoria's eyes widened slightly—they had made no such arrangement—but she placed her hand in his without hesitation. "Of course, darling."

As he led her onto the dance floor, Eustace told himself his racing pulse was from annoyance at having to maintain their facade. Not from the way she fit perfectly in his arms, or how her eyes sparkled with barely contained amusement.

"Jealous, Your Grace?" she whispered as they turned through the waltz.

"Don't be absurd," he muttered. "I'm simply maintaining our arrangement."

"Of course." Her smile was knowing. "Though I must say, you do an excellent impression of a possessive fiancé."

He grunted.

***

He picked up the rumpled note from the trash can.

Eustace might have missed it entirely had his butler not mentioned he'd seen her dispose of a letter that morning.

He unfolded and read it.

*Your secret won't stay hidden forever. Payment expected by week's end.*

His blood ran cold. Then hot with fury. Someone was threatening her—had been threatening her, perhaps for weeks while he'd been too blind to see it.

*Why?*

"Harrison," he called to his butler. "Have there been any... unusual visitors? Anyone asking after Her Ladyship?"

"Several rough-looking gentlemen have been observed near the servants' entrance, Your Grace. And..." Harrison hesitated. "Her Ladyship has been making frequent trips to the lower gardens, often returning quite distressed."

The pieces began falling into place—Vittoria's increasing anxiety, her disappearances, the mysterious men at their outings. How had he not seen it sooner? Did she have a lover?

That night, against every instinct of propriety and trust, Eustace followed her into the gardens. The moon cast long shadows as she hurried along the path, her dark cloak making her almost invisible in the darkness. She glanced over her shoulder twice, but never saw him.

Near the old gazebo, a figure waited. Male, from the breadth of his shoulders. Eustace's hand tightened on his walking stick, ready to intervene, when Vittoria reached into her reticule and handed something to the man—money, by the gleam of coins in the moonlight.

She was giving money to her lover?

"This is the last time," he heard her say, her voice trembling. "don't come back here. Stop the blackmail."

Blackmail. The word hit him like a physical blow. But before he could step forward, the man grabbed her arm.

"You'll pay what we ask, my darling, or you know what happens next."

Eustace froze.

He watched Vittoria wrench her arm free and hurry back toward the house, tears gleaming on her cheeks. And in that moment, standing alone in his darkened garden, Eustace wondered what to do.

## Chapter Eleven

Clara stared at her prized collection of silver needles, each one catching the morning light that filtered through her workshop window. These weren't just sewing supplies—they were pieces of her dream, carefully collected over years of scrimping and saving.

"Twenty pounds for the lot," Mr. Harrison said, his voice cutting through her memories. "And that's being generous, considering."

Considering what? That she was desperate? That everyone in the merchant district probably knew about her stepfamily's latest "visits"? Clara bit her tongue to keep the sharp retort from escaping.

The finest needle in her collection—the one she'd used to create three different duchesses' wedding gowns—caught a ray of sunlight. She remembered the day she'd bought it, how she'd gone without lunch for two weeks to afford it.

"Twenty-five," she said, lifting her chin. Even now, she wouldn't let them see her beg. "They're worth twice that new."

"Twenty-two."

Clara's fingers curled around the leather case holding her needles. She could almost hear her stepfather's mocking laugh. *Look at you now, playing at being a lady while selling off everything you've built.*

"Fine." The word tasted like ashes. "Twenty-two."

Mr. Harrison counted out the coins with deliberate slowness. Each clink against the wooden counter felt like another piece of her dignity falling away.

Not enough. It still wasn't enough to meet their demands.

Next would be her special-order silks. Then the lace she'd been saving for... well, it didn't matter now, did it?

"Pleasure doing business," Mr. Harrison said, already turning away with her precious needles.

Clara watched him go, her throat tight. *Don't cry. Don't you dare cry.*

She had four more stops to make before noon. The fancy silver scissors her first satisfied customer had gifted her. The rare pattern books from Paris. Even the little mechanical pincushion that had been her mother's.

*"Two thousand pounds,"* her stepfather's voice echoed in her head. *"Or everyone learns exactly what kind of fraud you are."*

Clara straightened her shoulders. She'd built herself from nothing once before. She could do it again if she had to.

But oh, how it hurt to watch another piece of her real life slip away, all to protect this fantasy she'd stumbled into.

The bell above the shop door chimed. Clara quickly wiped her eyes and turned, the practiced smile of Madame Celestine already in place.

Time to sell another piece of herself.

After all, what choice did she have?

Later that evening, notes from the pianoforte floated through Ravencroft House's music room like butterflies, delicate and perfect.

Clara sat among the assembled guests, her hands folded perfectly in her lap, her smile fixed in place.

Everything was fine. Everything was wonderful.

Until she saw him.

Thomas appeared in the doorway like a ghost from her nightmares, his broad shoulders stretching the limits of what must have been borrowed evening wear. Their eyes met across the room.

Clara's fingers dug into her fan. No. Not here. Not now.

"Are you enjoying the performance, my dear?" Duchess Dowager whispered from beside her.

"Oh yes," Clara managed, though the music had become nothing but noise in her ears. "Miss Peterson plays beautifully."

Thomas was moving through the crowd now, accepting a glass of wine from a servant as if he belonged here. As if he hadn't spent years mocking her for even dreaming of entering such rooms.

Think. She had to think.

"I believe I need some air," Clara murmured, rising as gracefully as she could manage. "The room is rather warm."

She made it halfway to the terrace before Thomas intercepted her, his meaty hand closing around her arm.

"Sister dear," he said, loud enough for nearby guests to hear. "How fortunate to find you here."

Clara's heart hammered against her ribs. "Remove your hand," she whispered through her smile, "or I'll scream."

"Now, now. Is that any way to treat family?"

"Is there a problem?"

Eustace's voice cut through the tension like a sword. He stood behind Thomas, every inch the powerful duke, his expression promising consequences.

Thomas's grip loosened. "No problem at all. Simply greeting my dear—"

"Leave." Eustace didn't raise his voice. He didn't have to. "Now."

Clara watched Thomas retreat, her arm burning where he'd grabbed her. She forced herself to breathe normally, to smile as if nothing had happened.

"An unwanted admirer?" Eustace asked quietly.

If only he knew. "Something like that." Clara smoothed her skirts, willing her hands to stop shaking. "Thank you for your intervention."

"Shall I have him removed from the guest list permanently?"

"Please." The word came out more desperate than she'd intended.

Eustace's eyes narrowed slightly, but he simply offered his arm. "Come. You're missing Miss Peterson's interpretation of Mozart."

Clara took his arm, letting him lead her back to the music room. Back to the facade of perfect contentment.

But even as she sat listening to the pianoforte, she could feel Thomas's presence lingering like a shadow. How much more would they demand? How much more could she give?

The music swelled to a crescendo, and Clara applauded with everyone else, her smile never wavering.

She was getting better at this, she realized. Better at pretending everything was fine while her world crumbled around her.

She just wasn't sure if that was something to be proud of.

\*\*\*

Days later, Clara stood before the cheval mirror in Lady Margaret's dressing room, hands trembling as she smoothed the fabric of the emerald green gown she'd just fitted to perfection.

For a moment, she let herself marvel at her handiwork. The gown hugged Margaret's slim frame, emphasizing her best features with an understated elegance that only Clara could achieve. But this wasn't just about appearances; it was about survival.

"Oh, Vittoria it's stunning!" Margaret turned, her cheeks flushed with joy. "You must have a magic touch."

Clara forced a smile. "I'm glad it pleases you. A dress should always make the wearer feel as though they can conquer the world."

She felt a pang in her chest as she spoke. How long had it been since she'd truly felt that way? Lately, her world seemed to shrink with every passing day, hemmed in by demands, secrets, and threats.

"Do you think Lord Barry will notice?" Margaret's voice carried a teasing note, her eyes sparkling as she twirled before the mirror.

Lord Barry was Lady's Margeret's new admirer, and she had been talking about how she wanted to impress the man all day.

Clara managed a light laugh. "He'd have to be blind not to."

Margaret beamed and reached out to clasp Clara's hands. "You're so talented, Vittoria. Truly. I can't imagine anyone else pulling off this transformation. Eustace is lucky to have you."

The words struck Clara like a blow. If Margaret only knew the truth. But instead of responding, Clara squeezed Margaret's hands, her smile brittle as she excused herself.

***

That evening, Clara took her place beside Eustace at the grand dining table, her spine ramrod straight, every inch the composed fiancée. The chandelier overhead glittered like a thousand stars, casting its light on the silverware and the polished faces of the guests. Clara felt as though she were on display, a fragile figurine waiting for the slightest tap to send her crashing to pieces.

Across the room, she caught sight of her stepfather, lurking just beyond the servants' entrance, his expression cold and calculating. He tilted his head slightly, a silent message that sent ice coursing through her veins. He was here to remind her of his power, his hold over her.

"Are you all right?" Eustace's low voice pulled her from her spiraling thoughts.

She turned to him, his dark eyes searching hers. For a fleeting moment, she considered telling him everything—about the blackmail, the threats, the suffocating weight of her double life.

But she couldn't. Not here. Not now.

"Of course," she lied smoothly, lifting her wine glass to her lips to hide her trembling.

He didn't look convinced, but thankfully, the conversation around them shifted, drawing his attention elsewhere.

\*\*\*

After dinner, Clara excused herself, slipping away from the gathering under the guise of needing fresh air. She made her way to the dimly lit staircase near the servants' quarters and slipped out the side door leading to the gardens, her heart pounding. She couldn't let this go on.

Her stepfather had to be stopped.

She waited, her palms damp, her breath shallow as she rehearsed what she would say. When she heard footsteps, she straightened, ready to confront him.

But it wasn't her stepfather who appeared.

"Lord Edmund," she breathed, her voice laced with dread.

He emerged from the shadows, his smirk cold and predatory. "Ah, Miss Mills. Or should I say...Madame Celestine? Or perhaps the faux Countess Romano?"

Clara stiffened, her mind racing. She couldn't afford to show weakness. "I don't know what you're talking about," she said, her tone icy.

"Oh, come now. Let's not play coy. I know who you are. And I know what you're not." He took a deliberate step closer, his gaze pinning her in place. "A little seamstress playing dress-up, aren't you? Tell me, how long did you think you could keep up this charade?"

Clara's breath hitched. "What do you want, Edmund?"

"I want you to confess." His voice was low, dangerous. "Tell everyone the truth, or I'll do it for you. And believe me, my version of the story will be far less kind."

Her knees nearly buckled. "Please," she whispered, hating the desperation in her voice but unable to mask it. "You don't understand. If you expose me, you'll destroy more than just me. Eustace—"

"Eustace will survive," Edmund cut her off with a sneer. "But you? You'll be ruined. Unless..."

Clara's heart seized. "Unless what?"

"Unless you disappear. Leave now, tonight. Go back to whatever hovel you crawled out of. Spare us all the scandal, and perhaps I'll spare you."

Tears burned at the corners of her eyes, but she blinked them back. "I can't do that."

"Then prepare to face the consequences."

Clara bit her lip, her voice breaking. "Please, Edmund. I'll do anything—just don't ruin me."

He stepped closer, so close she could feel his breath against her cheek. "Anything?"

Before she could respond, a shadow moved from behind the bushes, and a voice cut through the tension like a blade.

"That's quite enough, Edmund."

# Chapter Twelve

The grand dinner at Ravencroft Manor buzzed with life. The hum of conversation, the clink of crystal goblets, and the distant strains of a violinist's melody filled the space.

Eustace Montague stood near the hearth, his sharp gaze sweeping over the assembled guests.

He had no patience for the pomp of the evening, yet duty demanded his presence. His jaw tightened as he observed the room, but his mind was not on the revelry before him—it was on her.

Vittoria. The woman who was supposed to act as his betrothed.

She had disappeared again. For the third time that evening.

His grip on the crystal tumbler tightened. It was becoming a pattern—her frequent absences even while they were at public events, the hushed tones in which the servants spoke of her, and the peculiar unease that had begun to gnaw at his instincts.

Something about her was amiss, and it infuriated him to no end.

From the moment he had proposed this absurd engagement—meant solely to stave off his mother's and society's incessant meddling—Vittoria had proven to be both a complication and a distraction.

She was not the boring, quiet girl he remembered from years ago. Instead, she was...

*Different*. But at the same time, not different.

His frown deepened as he moved toward the door leading out of the hall.

This was their grand dinner; he couldn't allow anything to go wrong. He would find her.

***

Eustace's boots echoed softly against the polished marble floor as he prowled through the shadowed corridors of the manor.

The flickering light of wall sconces cast long, restless shadows that mirrored his unease.

He caught sight of a figure slipping around the corner ahead—a flash of a pale gown beneath a shawl.

Vittoria.

His pulse quickened, though he would never admit to himself why.

The idea that she might be meeting a clandestine lover coiled in his chest like a venomous serpent.

It was absurd, of course. Vittoria was far too clever and graceful for something so obvious.

But the thought of another man touching her, speaking to her in tones of intimacy, was intolerable.

He would put an end to it all tonight.

He reached the end of the corridor just in time to see her disappearing through a side door leading to the gardens.

Without hesitation, he followed.

The cold night air struck him, but he ignored it.

The scent of damp earth and late-blooming roses filled the air, but Eustace had no time for the beauty of the scene.

His focus was entirely on the figures ahead—her, and the man suddenly looming over her.

He drew to a halt, his frame instinctively stilling as he melted into the shadows.

His jaw clenched as his keen eyes took in the scene: Vittoria, standing before Edmund, her body tense, her hands clasped tightly at her waist.

"Please," she was saying, her voice low and strained. "You don't understand. If you expose me, you'll destroy more than just me. Eustace—"

"Eustace will survive." Edmund sneered. "But you? You'll be ruined... unless..."

Eustace's blood turned to ice.

What was happening?

His fists curled at his sides as he watched her face. She was pleading—genuine desperation etched into every line of her expression. He saw the predatory look in Edmund's eyes and saw red.

Her voice trembled as she said, "Unless what?"

Eustace's stomach tightened. A cold suspicion was beginning to take shape in his mind, one that left a bitter taste on his tongue.

"Unless you disappear. Leave now, tonight. Go back to whatever hovel you crawled out of. Spare us all the scandal, and perhaps I'll spare you." Edmund said with a smirk.

"I can't do that..." Clara's voice cracked, and Eustace froze. Not because of the word itself, but because of how she said it—with raw, unguarded fear.

He had never heard Vittoria speak like that.

*Because she isn't Vittoria, is she?*

Eustace's breath hissed out, and for a moment, he felt unmoored. The woman who had so thoroughly captured his thoughts, his desires, was not who she claimed to be.

She really was an imposter.

And yet, as he looked at her trembling figure, something else flared in his chest—something stronger than anger or betrayal.

Possession.

Whatever she had done, whoever she truly was, she was his.

Edmund stepped closer and Eustace snapped out of his thoughts.

The bastard was close to Vittoria—or whatever her name was. Too close.

"Anything?" He purred.

Eustace felt a sharp jolt of anger rip through him. His hands clenched into fists at his sides, his nails biting into his palms. The audacity of the man—standing on his property, threatening his woman—was nearly unbearable.

He'd had enough. "That's quite enough, Edmund."

Eustace's voice cut through the night like the slash of a blade. Both Clara and Edmund froze, their heads snapping toward him.

He stepped out of the shadows, his tall frame dominating the moonlit path. His dark eyes were fixed on Edmund, sharp as tempered steel.

The man's smirk faltered, but he recovered quickly, schooling his features into a mask of indifference. "Your Grace," he said, inclining his head. "I was merely—"

"Overstepping your bounds," Eustace finished coldly, his tone leaving no room for argument. He moved closer, his boots crunching against the gravel. "How curious that you find yourself skulking about my gardens, harassing my fiancée. Have you no sense of propriety?"

Edmund bristled, but he had the good sense to step back. "I assure you, I meant no harm. I was merely—"

"You were merely speaking out of turn," Eustace interrupted, his gaze narrowing. "And I have little patience for it."

"Your Grace," Edmund said, straightening his jacket as though to recover his composure. "You misunderstand. I was merely—"

"Do I need to repeat myself?" Eustace interjected, his voice as cold and sharp as the autumn air. His dark gaze pinned Edmund in place, daring him to argue. "I was not aware that you were appointed as my fiancée's interrogator. Unless I misremember?"

"No, of course not," Edmund muttered, but his tone was sour. His gaze flicked toward Clara, and Eustace didn't miss the slight curl of his lips—a lingering taunt that set Eustace's teeth on edge.

"Then I suggest you take your leave," Eustace said, his voice dropping an octave. He took a single, deliberate step forward, towering over the man. "Now."

Edmund's jaw tightened, but he bowed stiffly, clearly unwilling to test Eustace's patience further. "Good evening, Your Grace. Countess Vittoria."

Eustace's gaze remained fixed on him, unflinching, until the man turned and disappeared into the shadows of the garden. Only then did he shift his attention to Clara.

She stood rooted to the spot, her hands clasped tightly in front of her, her knuckles white against the fabric of her shawl.

Her breaths came shallow and quick, and the faint moonlight caught the sheen of unshed tears in her eyes.

Eustace felt a strange, unwelcome pang in his chest. Despite the deception—despite everything—seeing her so shaken stirred something in him that he couldn't ignore.

He didn't hate her. He found he couldn't. Instead, whatever he felt for her seemed to intensify.

"You look pale," he said, his voice softer but no less commanding. "Has he frightened you?"

"No," she said quickly, though her voice wavered. She lowered her gaze, clearly unwilling to meet his eyes. "It was nothing, Your Grace. A mere... disagreement."

Eustace arched a brow, stepping closer. "I find it difficult to believe that such a trivial matter would warrant the tone I overheard. Shall I summon Edmund back and demand an explanation?"

Her head snapped up, her eyes wide with alarm. "No!" she blurted, the word escaping her lips before she could stop it. She swallowed hard, her voice trembling as she added, "I mean, there's no need for that. Truly, Your Grace, it was nothing of importance."

Eustace studied her closely, his dark eyes narrowing. She was a poor liar—something that should have angered him, yet he found it almost endearing. She looked at him now as though he held the power to destroy her, and he wondered if she realized just how much power she held over him instead.

"Nothing of importance," he repeated slowly, his tone laced with skepticism. He let the words hang in the air, watching the way her lips parted, the way her hands fidgeted with the edge of her shawl.

"Precisely," she murmured, though she couldn't seem to meet his gaze.

The silence stretched between them, thick with tension. Eustace should have left it there—should have turned on his heel and walked back into the manor, leaving her to stew in her secrets. But something kept him rooted in place.

He took another step closer, until the faint scent of her—something soft and floral, maddeningly subtle—reached him. "If that is the case, then you will not mind telling me what precisely has unsettled you so."

Her lips trembled, and for a fleeting moment, he thought she might tell him the truth. But then she shook her head, her voice barely above a whisper. "I cannot."

Eustace's jaw tightened, but he forced himself to remain calm. "Very well," he said, though his tone was clipped. "You are under my protection now—"

He paused, not knowing what to call her. Madame Celeste?

"—Vittoria. If there is trouble, you will inform me of it. Do you understand?"

She nodded mutely, though her expression was guarded.

"Good," he said curtly, though his frustration simmered just beneath the surface. "Now, let us return to the manor. It is far too cold for you to linger here."

She hesitated, as though debating whether to argue, but eventually she nodded and turned toward the house.

Eustace walked beside her, his gaze lingering on the graceful line of her neck, the way the moonlight caught the soft curves of her figure.

Goodness... She was a liar, an imposter, a puzzle he had yet to solve. And yet, against all logic, he found himself wanting to unravel her—not to expose her, but to understand her.

He would get his answers. One way or another.

***

Eustace walked a step behind Clara as they made their way back to the manor, his hands clasped behind his back and his gaze fixed on her. The quiet rustle of her skirts against the gravel mingled with the faint murmur of the wind through the trees.

She hadn't spoken since they'd left the garden, her shoulders tense and her head slightly bowed, as though retreating into her thoughts.

He couldn't stop watching her.

It wasn't her beauty alone that held his attention—though he would be a liar if he denied its pull. There was something else, something in the delicate line of her profile and the way she carried herself.

She wasn't pretending now; she was simply herself.

And it struck him that it was this version of her that had captured him so entirely. It was this version of her when the countess was younger that made him beg his parents for her hand in marriage no matter how small they were.

As they passed the rear of the manor, a young maid darted across their path, her arms full of freshly laundered linens. The girl stumbled, her face flushing with embarrassment as she hastily stepped aside to make way.

"Your pardon, Your Grace, Countess Vittoria," the maid stammered, her head bowed.

Before Eustace could respond, she turned to the girl, her voice warm and gentle. "There is nothing to pardon, Mary. Are those for the nursery?"

The maid blinked in surprise, nodding. "Yes, lady."

"Be careful on the stairs, won't you? That bundle looks heavy," she said with a smile.

The maid hesitated, as though unsure how to respond, then bobbed a quick curtsey and hurried on her way. Eustace watched the scene unfold in silence, his brow furrowing. Her tone, her kindness—it was unforced, entirely natural.

His mind couldn't help but draw comparisons. The real Vittoria had never bothered to learn the servants' names, let alone speak to them with such care. To her, they were invisible, just like every other person was to her.

And yet this Vittoria—this woman who had deceived him—was nothing like that cold, haughty girl from his youth.

Further along, a small figure darted from the shadows, nearly colliding with them. A boy of about eight, one of the kitchen lads, skidded to a halt in front of Clara, his face smeared with soot.

"Beggin' yer pardon, Miss!" the boy panted, clutching a toy soldier in one hand.

Clara crouched before him, her skirts pooling around her, and smiled. "What's this, Jack? Playing soldier again?"

The boy nodded eagerly, his embarrassment fading under her attention. "Aye, Lady. Cook sent me out to fetch the coal, but I couldn't leave him behind." He held up the wooden toy as though it were a prized treasure.

Clara laughed softly. "A wise decision. Every good soldier needs his companion. Now hurry along before Cook starts looking for you, hmm?"

The boy grinned and darted off, his steps light and quick.

Eustace stared after the lad, his chest tightening inexplicably. Vittoria wouldn't have spared a second glance at the child, much less crouched in her fine gown to speak to him.

He found himself flooded with memories of the real Vittoria: her cutting remarks, her uncaring attitude for those beneath her station, her cold beauty that had repelled more than it enticed. And here was this woman—deceitful, yes, but so utterly different that it felt like he was seeing her for the first time.

She wasn't Vittoria.

And he was glad for it.

He realized, with startling clarity, that his original plan—the calculated game of a fake engagement—was no longer enough. Somewhere along the way, his indifference had been replaced by something else, something far more dangerous.

Something real.

He stopped abruptly, his boots crunching against the gravel. "Vittoria."

She froze mid-step, then turned to face him, her expression cautious. "Yes, Your Grace?"

He stepped closer, his dark eyes searching hers. "I find I no longer have the patience for pretense."

Her brows furrowed, confusion flickering across her face. "I... I don't understand."

"Then allow me to make myself clear," he said, his voice low and steady. "I no longer wish to continue this charade of an engagement. I will not lie to my family, to society, or to myself. What I want now is something real. A true relationship. With you."

Her lips parted, her eyes widening in shock. For a moment, she seemed unable to respond, her gaze darting away as though searching for some escape.

"Your Grace, I..." Her voice faltered, and she looked back at him, her expression a mixture of panic and disbelief. "You cannot mean that."

"I do," he said simply.

"You don't understand," she whispered, shaking her head. "You don't know—"

"I know enough," he interrupted, his tone firm but soft. "Enough to see that you are the one I want."

Her breath hitched, and for a fleeting moment, he thought she might cry. But then she took a step back, her arms crossing over her chest as though to shield herself.

"This is impossible," she murmured. "You don't even know me."

"Perhaps not," he admitted. "But I know what I feel. And I know that whatever this is, it's worth pursuing."

She shook her head again, her voice breaking. "No, Your Grace. We can't. This—this cannot happen."

She was trembling. He could see it in the way her shoulders rose and fell, in the way her hands clutched the edge of the curtain.

"Vittoria," he said softly, his deep voice breaking the silence.

She turned sharply at the sound of her name, her face pale but her eyes blazing with emotion. "Your Grace," she said, her voice strained, "I told you this cannot happen. Please, don't make this harder than it already is."

Eustace's brow furrowed, his frustration bubbling beneath the surface. "Harder? For whom? You claim this cannot happen, yet you offer no reason. I am not a man accustomed to accepting refusals without explanation."

Her lips pressed into a thin line, and she turned away again, shaking her head. "You wouldn't understand."

"Then make me understand," he demanded, his voice rising ever so slightly. He took another step forward, his presence filling the room. "You think I do not see you? That I do not see the woman who has bewitched me with her every smile, her every word?"

"Stop!" she cried, spinning to face him. Her voice cracked, and tears glistened in her eyes. "Stop saying such things! You shouldn't... you can't feel that way about me."

Eustace froze, her anguish cutting through him like a blade. For a moment, he was silent, his dark eyes studying her face. Her distress was genuine, raw, and it only deepened the ache in his chest.

"And why not?" he asked quietly, his tone softening. "Tell me, Vittoria. Why can I not feel what I feel for you?"

"Because I am unworthy of you!" she burst out, her voice breaking as the first tear slipped down her cheek. She wiped at it furiously, as though angry at her own weakness. "You deserve someone of your station, someone flawless, someone who hasn't—" she shook her head.

Eustace's jaw tightened. He wanted to tell her he knew the truth, that he'd overheard everything. But the vulnerability in her eyes held him back. For now, he would let her keep her secret.

"Unworthy?" he echoed, his voice low and laced with disbelief. He took another step forward, closing the distance between them. "You speak as though you have the right to determine my worth. As though you can dictate what I may or may not desire."

Her tears fell freely now, her hands trembling as she tried to push him away—not physically, but with her words. "Please, Your Grace. I'm begging you. This cannot happen. You will only regret it, and so will I."

Eustace's patience snapped. He stepped forward, closing the remaining space between them, and cupped her face in his hands. Her skin was warm and soft beneath his touch, her tears dampening his fingers.

"Enough," he said firmly, his voice a low growl. "If you believe I will stand here and let you tear yourself down, you are gravely mistaken."

Her breath hitched, her eyes wide as she looked up at him. He could see the battle waging within her, the fear and longing that clashed behind those luminous eyes.

"Eustace," she whispered, her voice barely audible.

He didn't give her a chance to say more. Leaning down, he captured her lips with his in a kiss that was both tender and unyielding. It wasn't just a kiss—it was a declaration, a promise, a demand. He poured every ounce of his passion, his frustration, his longing into it, willing her to feel what he could not yet put into words.

For a brief, glorious moment, she responded. Her lips softened against his, and her hands clutched the lapels of his coat as though anchoring herself. It was everything he had imagined and more—a connection that left him breathless, a fire that ignited his very soul.

But just as quickly as it began, it ended.

She tore herself away, her breath ragged and her cheeks flushed. "I'm sorry," she choked out, tears streaming down her face. "I can't... I can't do this."

Before he could stop her, she turned and fled, her skirts billowing behind her as she disappeared into the night.

Eustace stood frozen, his chest heaving and his heart pounding. The taste of her lingered on his lips, and his hands ached from the memory of her warmth.

She had run, but he would not let her go.

He swore then and there that he would uncover every truth she hid from him, that he would break down every wall she built between them.

And he would protect her with all he had.

# Chapter Thirteen

Clara sat by the window, staring out into the moonlit gardens of Ravencroft House. The world looked so peaceful, but her heart was anything but. Her stepfather's latest threats still rang in her ears, as sharp and cruel as the man himself.

Her fingers gripped the edge of her sewing basket, the place where she kept her most treasured belongings—small reminders of the life she'd built with her own hands. The life she was about to lose.

She couldn't stay. Not with Edmund sniffing around, her stepfamily's demands piling higher by the day, and now... now there was Eustace.

Eustace. The name alone sent a storm of emotions crashing through her. She thought of the way he'd looked at her last night after Edmund cornered her. The fury in his eyes when he'd told Edmund off, his arm protectively around her as if she truly were his.

It had been too much. Too close. She couldn't keep pretending, couldn't let this charade go on a moment longer. But the thought of leaving him, of walking away forever, made her chest ache in ways she couldn't explain.

Her decision had been made, though. She had to leave. The longer she stayed, the more dangerous this became—for both of them.

But before she left, there was one thing she couldn't run from. He deserved the truth. He deserved to know who she was and why she'd deceived him.

Clara rose from her seat, her fingers trembling as she smoothed the front of her dress. The soft cotton felt cool beneath her touch, grounding her as she paced the room. She had no idea how to begin, no idea how to explain everything without shattering the fragile trust between them.

And then there were the wishes.

She hadn't planned them, not really. They'd just come to her in a burst of desperate longing—three moments she wanted to share with him before everything fell apart.

It was foolish, really, to want something so sentimental when she'd spent her entire life surviving on practicality. But if she was going to say goodbye, she wanted it to be meaningful.

She glanced at the clock. Eustace would be back soon. She'd already rehearsed what she wanted to say a dozen times, but somehow it never felt right.

Taking a deep breath, she began to tidy the room, her movements quick and nervous. The embroidered pillows on the settee had to be perfectly arranged. The book on the desk needed to sit at just the right angle.

The room had to look as perfect as she pretended to be.

When the sound of footsteps reached her ears, Clara froze. Her heart raced as the door creaked open, and there he was—Eustace, tall and imposing, his dark eyes locking onto hers the moment he stepped inside.

She couldn't look at him without feeling the weight of everything she was about to confess. But Clara straightened her shoulders, determined to hold onto the last shred of dignity she had left.

Clara clasped her hands tightly in front of her, forcing herself to appear calm, though her heart was a frantic mess beneath her bodice.

"Vittoria?" His voice was low, steady, but edged with something cautious. "Why are you sitting here in the dark?"

She stiffened. Vittoria. Not Clara. Not by her supposed given name.

"I... I needed a moment," she replied, her voice softer than she intended.

He stepped closer, studying her with an intensity that made her feel far too exposed. "You look as though you've seen a ghost."

She gave a tight, unconvincing laugh. "Nonsense."

But Eustace didn't look convinced. He stopped a few feet away, crossing his arms as he leaned against the mantel. The firelight flickered across his face, highlighting the strong line of his jaw and the furrow in his brow.

"What's wrong, Vittoria?"

"Nothing," she said quickly, too quickly. She couldn't look at him for long without her composure cracking.

His silence dragged on, and Clara felt her chest tighten under the weight of it. He was watching her, waiting for her to slip, to say something that would give away the chaos raging inside her.

Finally, he spoke, his voice quieter now but no less firm. "I know you better than that. You've been avoiding me for days, sneaking away at odd hours, and tonight you're sitting here, pale as a sheet, like you're about to run."

Her breath caught. "I'm not—"

"Don't lie to me."

The words were gentle but left no room for argument. Eustace pushed off the mantel, closing the distance between them. His height towered over her as he bent slightly, trying to catch her eyes.

Clara hated how easily he saw through her, how his steady gaze seemed to strip away every layer of her defenses.

"I—" Her throat tightened, and she shook her head. "I need you to grant me three wishes."

His brow furrowed deeper. "Three wishes?"

"Yes." She squared her shoulders, even as her fingers fidgeted with the fabric of her dress. "Before I leave."

Eustace went still, his expression unreadable. For a moment, she thought he might walk away, might dismiss her request as the desperate ramblings of a woman on the edge.

But then he straightened, his arms falling to his sides. "Three wishes," he repeated, his voice softer now, almost resigned. "You're really going to leave."

Clara looked away, unable to face the emotions she saw flicker across his face. "Yes."

A beat of silence passed between them before he stepped even closer, close enough that she could feel the warmth radiating from him.

"All right," he said, his voice rough. "What's your first wish?"

Clara's breath hitched. She hadn't expected him to agree so easily, hadn't expected the sadness in his voice.

"I want to go to the lake," she said, her words barely above a whisper. "With you."

He frowned, as though the simplicity of her request puzzled him. But he nodded, offering his hand. "Then let's go."

\*\*\*

The walk to the lake was quieter than Clara had imagined it would be. She couldn't bring herself to speak, too consumed by the weight of what she'd just set into motion. Eustace didn't press her for answers, but she could feel his gaze flicking toward her every so often, as though he was trying to read her thoughts.

When they reached the edge of the water, Clara stopped, her breath catching at the sight before her. The moonlight painted the lake in shades of silver, the surface so still it looked like glass. The trees around them rustled softly in the night breeze, their leaves shimmering like stars.

"It's beautiful," she said, her voice barely audible.

Eustace stood beside her, his hands tucked into his pockets. "I used to come here as a boy," he said after a moment. "Whenever the world felt too loud. This was the only place that made sense."

She turned to him, surprised by the vulnerability in his tone. He wasn't looking at her but at the lake, his gaze distant, as though he was remembering something long buried.

"I can see why," she said, offering a small smile.

He glanced at her then, and the look in his eyes made her heart twist.

"Is this what you wanted?" he asked quietly.

Clara nodded, though she wasn't sure if she meant the lake or something far less tangible.

They stood there for a while, the silence between them oddly comforting. Clara wished she could freeze this moment, hold onto it forever. But time was slipping through her fingers, and she couldn't afford to linger in her fantasies.

When she finally spoke, her voice was shaky but determined. "My second wish..." She hesitated, her cheeks flushing with heat.

Eustace turned to her, his brows lifting slightly. "What is it?"

"I want to dance," she said quickly, before she could change her mind. "With you. Just once. No pretending, no audience. Just us."

For a moment, she thought he might refuse. But then he held out his hand, his expression unreadable.

"Just us," he said softly.

Clara's heart raced as she placed her hand in his, his warmth seeping into her skin. He guided her gently, his other hand resting lightly on her waist as he began to move.

There was no music, just the soft rustle of the wind and the quiet lapping of the water. But it didn't matter. Eustace's movements were fluid and confident, his steps guiding hers as though they'd danced together a thousand times before.

Clara felt her walls begin to crumble, piece by piece. She wanted to hate how easy it was to fall into rhythm with him, how perfectly they fit together.

"You're quiet," he said after a moment, his voice a low murmur.

"I'm trying to remember this," she replied honestly. "Every second of it."

Eustace's hand tightened slightly on her waist, and she wondered if he was doing the same.

When the dance finally ended, Clara stepped back, her chest tight with emotions she couldn't name.

Eustace didn't release her hand right away, his fingers brushing against hers as he searched her face.

"There's something you're not telling me," he said, his voice soft but insistent.

Clara's breath caught. For a moment, she considered telling him everything right then and there. But she couldn't. Not yet.

"Thank you," she said instead, her voice trembling. "For granting my wishes."

He frowned, clearly unsatisfied with her evasion. But he didn't push her further.

"Two wishes down," he said quietly. "What's the third?"

She turned to face Eustace, her heart pounding as her breath hitched. The night was quiet, save for the distant roll of thunder that rumbled across the horizon.

"My final wish," she began, her voice soft but clear, "is to hear you say my name."

Eustace frowned, confused by the request. "Your name?"

"Yes," she said, holding his gaze. "Not Countess. Not Vittoria. My name."

"I say your name all the time," he replied, his voice quiet but firm.

Clara shook her head, taking a hesitant step closer. "No, not Vittoria. My real name."

The words hung between them, fragile and raw, as the first drops of rain began to fall.

Eustace's confusion gave way to something sharper, something deeper. His eyes narrowed, and he took a step toward her. "What are you saying?"

Clara's throat tightened, but she forced herself to speak. "I'm saying that Vittoria Romano is not my name. It never was."

He stared at her, the realization dawning slowly, painfully. His voice dropped, barely audible over the increasing patter of the rain. "Then who are you?"

She hesitated, every part of her screaming to run, to hide, to bury the truth. But she couldn't anymore. Not with him.

"My name is Clara Mills," she said, her voice trembling. "I'm not a countess. I'm not anyone important. I'm just... a seamstress. A liar."

The words fell from her lips like stones, heavy and unforgiving. She braced herself for his reaction, for the anger, the disbelief, the betrayal.

But Eustace didn't move. His dark eyes remained locked on hers, his expression unreadable as the rain began to soak through his coat, his hair falling in damp strands against his forehead.

Her voice cracked on the last word, and she couldn't bring herself to look at him. She expected anger, betrayal, maybe even disgust.

"Clara..." He said her name for the first time, and the sound of it sent a shiver through her. It was strange, hearing her real name in his voice, both unfamiliar and heartbreakingly intimate.

She took a step back, shaking her head. "I never meant for this to happen. I never meant to deceive you, or anyone. I was just trying to survive. And then... then everything spiraled out of control."

He closed the distance between them in two strides, his hands gripping her arms, not painfully but firmly enough to keep her from retreating further. "Why didn't you tell me?"

"Because I was afraid!" The words burst out of her, raw and desperate. "Afraid of what would happen if you knew, afraid of losing... everything."

His grip loosened slightly, but he didn't let her go. The rain was falling harder now, soaking them both to the skin, but neither seemed to notice.

"You should have trusted me," he said, his voice quieter now, tinged with something she couldn't quite name.

"I couldn't," she said, tears mixing with the rain on her cheeks. "I couldn't trust anyone. Not with this."

For a long moment, they stood there, the storm raging around them as the weight of her confession settled between them.

Finally, Eustace let out a heavy breath, his hands dropping to his sides. "Why are you telling me now?"

"Because I'm leaving," she said, her voice barely audible. "After tonight, I'll be gone. And you'll never have to see me again."

His head snapped up, his eyes blazing with anger and something else—something that made her stomach twist. "You think you can just walk away? After everything?"

"I don't have a choice," she said, her voice breaking. "If I stay, it'll destroy both of us."

Eustace stepped closer again, his voice low and dangerous. "Don't you dare decide what's best for me. Don't you dare walk away without letting me have a say."

"I'm doing this for you!" she cried, the words ripping from her chest. "Don't you see that? If I stay, you'll lose everything—your reputation, your future, your—"

"You," he interrupted, his voice cutting through her like a blade. "I'll lose you."

The rain was relentless now, soaking through every layer of her dress, plastering her hair to her face. But Clara couldn't move, couldn't breathe, as he reached out, his fingers brushing her cheek.

"Eustace," she began, but he silenced her with a kiss.

It wasn't gentle. It was fierce and desperate, filled with everything he couldn't say. His hands cupped her face, pulling her closer as though he could keep her from slipping away. Clara's heart shattered as she kissed him back, her hands gripping his coat as if holding on for dear life.

When they finally pulled apart, their breaths ragged, Eustace rested his forehead against hers. "Don't leave," he whispered, his voice raw. "Stay. Fight. With me."

Tears streamed down her face, mixing with the rain. "I can't."

"You can," he said, his voice firm. "We can figure this out together. I don't care who you are, Clara. I don't care about the lies, or the past. All I care about is you."

Her chest ached with the force of her emotions. She wanted so badly to believe him, to let herself fall into the safety of his words.

But the reality of her situation loomed over her like a dark cloud. "You'll regret this," she whispered.

"Never." His voice was steady, unwavering.

Clara searched his eyes, looking for any hint of doubt. But all she saw was determination, fierce and unrelenting.

For a moment, she let herself believe him. Let herself imagine what it would be like to stay, to fight, to let herself love him without fear.

But she couldn't.

"I'm sorry," she said, her voice breaking as she stepped back.

"Clara—"

"I have to go."

Eustace stepped closer, his presence overwhelming. "Clara..."

She shook her head, cutting him off. "Don't. Please don't make this harder than it already is."

"I can't stay," she whispered, her voice barely audible.

"You don't have to run," he said, his eyes burning with determination. "Not from me."

# Chapter Fourteen

Rain continued to pour, soaking through Eustace's overcoat as he stood before her, the relentless storm matching the tempest inside him.

He couldn't let her leave. Not now. Not ever.

Clara's shoulders shook with silent sobs, her face streaked with tears that mingled with the rain. She was a vision of despair, yet to him, she was still utterly captivating. Every instinct he possessed urged him to pull her into his arms, to shield her from the world that had made her so afraid.

"Clara," he said, his voice low and firm, "you don't have to do this."

She shook her head, her hand clutching the small satchel she had packed. "I do. You don't understand."

"You're right," he admitted, taking a step closer. "I don't understand why you would run from the one place where you are safe. From the one person who would move heaven and earth to protect you."

Her lips parted, but no words came. Instead, she stared at him, her eyes glistening with pain and confusion. Eustace felt his heart constrict, a foreign ache that he had never thought himself capable of feeling.

"I am not a man prone to begging," he continued, his tone sharper now, his frustration bleeding through. "But I am begging you, Clara. Do not walk away from me."

Her chest heaved as she struggled to control her emotions. "Why?" she asked, her voice trembling. "Why would you want me to stay? You still don't even know who I really am."

He took another step forward, closing the gap between them until only inches separated them. "I know enough," he said, his gaze piercing hers. "I know that you are not Vittoria, but I also know that you are the woman who has consumed my thoughts, the woman who has made me feel things I swore I never would. Does that not matter to you at all?"

Her breath hitched, and she looked away, as though his words were too much to bear. "You'll regret this," she whispered, echoing the same words she had spoken before.

"Regret?" he echoed softly. "Do you take me for a fool, Clara? Do you think I do not know my own mind? I may have been blind to many things, but not to you. Never to you."

She turned back to him then, her expression torn between hope and despair. "It's not that simple."

"It is," he insisted, his voice dropping to a near-growl. "You make it complicated with your doubts and your running. But it is simple, Clara. I want you. Here. With me."

For a long moment, the only sound was the steady patter of rain around them. Clara seemed frozen, her satchel slipping from her fingers to the muddy ground.

"Stay," Eustace said, his voice softer now, almost pleading. "Just until the morning. I have something to show you—something important."

Her eyes searched his, as though trying to find a reason to say no. Instead, she nodded, her movements hesitant but resolute. "Until morning," she murmured.

Relief flooded through him, though he dared not show it. He reached out and took her hand, the chill of her skin a sharp reminder of how fragile this moment was.

"Come," he said, his tone gruff as he led her back toward the manor.

Inside, the warmth of the drawing room greeted them, the fire crackling in the hearth. Eustace watched as Clara stood by the flames, her damp dress clinging to her form, her arms wrapped around herself. She looked so small, so lost, and it tore at something deep within him.

"You're shivering," he said, moving to her side. Without waiting for permission, he removed his overcoat and draped it over her shoulders.

"Thank you," she whispered, her voice barely audible.

He didn't respond. Instead, he stood there, watching her with an intensity he couldn't suppress. Her lashes were heavy with rain, her cheeks flushed from the cold, and yet she had never looked more beautiful.

"Eustace," she said after a moment, turning to face him. "Why are you doing this?"

He frowned. "Because it is the only thing that makes sense to me."

She stared at him, her expression unreadable. "And if I leave in the morning?"

"You won't," he said with quiet conviction.

Clara opened her mouth to protest, but he silenced her with a look.

"Enough for tonight. Rest, Clara."

\*\*\*

In her chamber, Lucy, the lady's maid, helped Clara out of her sodden garments with practiced efficiency. The older woman clucked her tongue in motherly concern as she wrapped her mistress in warm linens.

"There now, my lady," Lucy murmured, helping Clara into a fresh nightgown. "Let's get you warm and settled before you catch your death."

Clara's protests were weak, her exhaustion evident as Lucy guided her to the bed. The maid drew the covers up around her, adding another blanket for good measure.

Outside the chamber door, Eustace stood with his arms crossed, every muscle tense with concern. Only when Lucy emerged did he let out the breath he'd been holding.

"She's sleeping now, my lord," Lucy assured him in hushed tones. "Poor thing was nearly asleep before her head touched the pillow."

Eustace nodded, his jaw tight. "You'll stay with her through the night?"

"Of course, my lord. I'll not leave her side."

He retreated to his study, but sleep proved elusive. The firelight flickered across the empty chair where she had sat just hours before, and Eustace made a silent vow. He would do whatever it took to keep her. To show her that she was his, not as part of some pretense, but as the very heart of his world.

When dawn's first light crept through the windows, he was already pacing the corridor. Lucy appeared with perfect timing, as if sensing his presence.

"She's still sleeping peacefully, my lord," the maid reported with a knowing smile. "And yes, she remained here all night."

The relief that flooded through him was profound. Clara was here, safe under his roof. And today, he would prove to her just how much she meant to him.

Now, in the quiet stillness of the morning as he entered her chamber along with Lucy, the truth struck him with the force of a gale. This—her in front of him, safe and close—was what he wanted. Not for a night, not for a fleeting moment, but forever.

Eustace, the Duke of Ravencroft, who had long scoffed at the idea of love or marriage, found himself completely undone by this woman who was not who she claimed to be, yet more real to him than anyone else had ever been.

She stirred, her lashes fluttering before her eyes opened. The moment her gaze met his, the fragile peace of the morning fractured.

"Eustace?" she whispered, her voice thick with sleep and confusion.

He straightened slightly, reluctant to break the connection but knowing he must. "Good morning, Clara."

She blinked, then seemed to remember where she was—and who she was with. She pulled back quickly, sitting up and clutching the blankets to her chest. "I—"

"You stayed," he said simply, his voice steady though his heart was anything but.

Her expression wavered, guilt and uncertainty battling in her eyes. "Only because you wouldn't let me leave," she said, her tone defensive.

"And I won't let you leave now, either," he replied, standing and stretching with a calmness he didn't entirely feel. "Not yet."

Her brows furrowed. "Eustace, what are you planning?"

He turned to face her, his dark eyes meeting hers with an intensity that silenced whatever protest she was about to make. "Trust me, Clara. By the end of today, everything will make sense."

Her lips parted as if to argue, but she closed them again, her shoulders slumping in defeat. "You're frustrating, do you know that?"

He allowed a small, wry smile. "I've been told."

***

An hour later, they were in the carriage, the countryside rolling past them in shades of green and gold. The atmosphere inside was tense, charged with the weight of unspoken words. Clara sat across from him, her posture rigid as she stared out the window, her fingers twisting in her lap.

"Are you going to tell me where we're going?" she asked at last, breaking the silence.

"No," he said, his tone annoyingly nonchalant.

Her head snapped toward him, her eyes narrowing. "You dragged me out of the manor at an ungodly hour, forced me into a carriage, and refuse to tell me why?"

"Precisely."

Her mouth opened, then closed, a huff of exasperation escaping her. "You are impossible."

"I've been called worse," he said, his lips twitching with the barest hint of amusement.

She glared at him, but the effect was softened by the faint flush that colored her cheeks. He found himself watching her too closely—the way the morning light caught the strands of her hair, the way her lips pressed together in frustration.

"Eustace," she said, her voice more serious now. "Please, just tell me what you're planning. If this is some kind of game—"

"It is not a game," he interrupted, his tone suddenly grave. "You will see soon enough."

Her brows knitted, uncertainty flickering across her face. "You're being cryptic on purpose, aren't you?"

"Perhaps."

She sighed, leaning back against the seat with a shake of her head. "You are insufferable."

"And yet, here you are," he said smoothly.

She didn't respond, but the way she looked out the window, her expression troubled, made his chest tighten. He wanted to reach across the space between them, to reassure her, but he knew she would not welcome it. Not yet.

\*\*\*

The carriage slowed as they approached an inn, a grand structure nestled against the backdrop of rolling hills. Clara's gaze shifted to him, her wariness clear.

"An inn?" she asked, her voice laced with confusion.

"Patience," he said as the carriage came to a stop.

He stepped out first, extending a hand to help her down. She hesitated for a fraction of a second before placing her hand in his, her touch sending a jolt through him.

Inside, the innkeeper greeted them with a deep bow, leading them to a private room at the back. Clara's grip on Eustace's arm tightened as they walked, her unease growing with each step.

"Eustace," she said under her breath, "what is this?"

"You will see," he replied, his tone softer now, though the weight of the moment pressed heavily on him.

As they reached the door, he paused, his hand on the latch. Turning to her, he held her gaze, his expression unreadable.

"Whatever happens, Clara," he said quietly, "remember that I am on your side."

Before she could respond, he opened the door.

Inside, a woman stood by the window, her posture regal, her dress immaculate. At the sound of their entrance, she turned, and Clara gasped.

## Chapter Fifteen

When the door to the private room creaked open, Clara's heart had stopped.

She stood frozen on the threshold, her breath caught in her throat as her gaze landed on the figure inside.

Even now as she stared, she couldn't understand it.

A woman—seated in an armchair by the window, her profile lit softly by the afternoon sun filtering through the lace curtains.

Clara blinked, gripping the edge of the doorframe for support. Her mind couldn't make sense of what she was seeing.

When the woman turned her head at the sound of the door, and Clara's world tilted all over again.

It made no sense.

It was like staring into a mirror, but one warped by subtle differences. The face was hers—her sharp cheekbones, her wide eyes, even the delicate curve of her jawline. But where Clara was always animated, always teetering between laughter and sass, this woman looked still.

Serene. Her pale blue dress was tailored with precision, and every strand of her blonde hair was pinned immaculately in place.

"Vittoria," Eustace had said from behind her some moments ago, his voice calm but deliberate, as if he were easing her into the shock. "Meet Clara."

The woman rose gracefully, and for a moment, the room felt too small, the air too thin. Clara couldn't move, couldn't breathe. She was staring at herself, or at least some impossibly refined version of herself.

"Clara," Eustace's voice pulled her back to reality. "Come in."

Her feet didn't feel like her own as she stepped inside. Her pulse pounded in her ears, drowning out the soft rustle of Vittoria's skirts as the woman moved toward her.

When they were just a few steps apart, Clara's breath faltered.

The resemblance was uncanny.

Eustace stepped aside, allowing Clara to take in the sight before her. Her heart thundered in her chest, the weight of what was happening settled over her.

"Clara," Eustace said softly, "meet the Countess Vittoria."

The air in the room felt heavy, charged with a tension that seemed to thrum against the walls. Eustace stood near the door, his tall frame motionless as he watched Clara take in the sight before her. Her reaction was exactly as he had anticipated: shock, confusion, and something deeper, something he couldn't yet name.

Clara stepped forward, her breath coming in uneven bursts. "Who... who is she?" Her voice was barely above a whisper, laced with disbelief.

Eustace allowed the silence to linger, knowing the weight of it would press on both women. Finally, he spoke, his deep voice cutting through the tension like a blade. "Clara, this is the Countess Vittoria."

The name hit the air like a thunderclap, and Clara turned to him, her eyes wide. "The countess?" she repeated, her voice trembling. "But... she looks..."

"Remarkably like you," Eustace finished for her, his dark gaze steady.

"Yes."

The countess took a measured step closer, her eyes narrowing as she studied Clara. There was no mistaking the resemblance: the same delicate bone structure, the same fiery undertones in their hair, though Vittoria's was styled to perfection while Clara's tumbled in soft waves. Yet their expressions could not have been more different—Vittoria's sharp and calculating, Clara's open and filled with questions.

"This is absurd," Vittoria said at last, her tone clipped. "Who is this woman, Your Grace, and why have you brought me here?"

Eustace inclined his head slightly, his hands clasped behind his back in a gesture of control. "This, Countess, is Clara," he said, his voice cool but firm. "The woman who has been masquerading as you these past weeks."

Clara's gasp was audible, her hands flying to her mouth. She turned back to Eustace, her eyes brimming with confusion and betrayal. "You knew the whole time?"

His expression softened, though he did not move. "I knew."

Her voice broke as she whispered, "For how long?"

"Long enough," he admitted, his gaze unwavering.

Clara took a step back, her movements halting as if the very ground beneath her had become unstable. "Why didn't you say anything?"

Eustace's jaw tightened, the raw emotions he had buried threatening to surface. "Because I needed to understand. And now, so do you."

The countess's sharp voice interrupted. "This is outrageous. You mean to tell me that this... this girl has been living in my place? Using my name?"

Eustace's head snapped toward her, his voice hardening. "She has done so out of necessity, Countess, not malice. There are circumstances you do not yet know."

Vittoria's lips pursed, but she said nothing further. Instead, her gaze shifted back to Clara, who seemed to shrink under the scrutiny.

"You really do look like me," Vittoria said, her tone less accusatory now and more curious, almost guilty even. She took a cautious step closer, her sharp eyes scanning Clara's face. "But not quite."

Clara flinched as Vittoria reached out, a gloved hand brushing against her cheek. The countess's expression remained unreadable, though her eyes seemed to darken with something akin to unease.

"This is impossible," Vittoria murmured. "I have no sisters. No family who would..." She trailed off, her words hanging in the air like an unspoken accusation.

Clara finally found her voice, though it was shaky. "I don't know why we look alike," she said, her words tumbling out in a rush. "I don't understand any of this."

Eustace stepped forward then, his presence commanding as he positioned himself between the two women. "That is precisely why we are here," he said, his voice steady. "There is a reason for this resemblance, and I intend to uncover it."

Clara's eyes darted to him, her vulnerability plain. "Eustace, what if there isn't? What if it's just some cruel coincidence?"

"Do you truly believe that?" he asked, his tone softening.

She hesitated, her gaze dropping to the floor. "No," she admitted quietly.

The countess crossed her arms, her composure slipping into something more human. "I don't like mysteries, Your Grace. And this one feels far too convenient."

Eustace turned to her, his expression impassive. "Convenient or not, it is a mystery that requires answers. And you, Countess, are an essential part of that."

Vittoria raised a brow but said nothing. Instead, she stepped back, her posture tense as she regarded Clara once more.

The two women stood facing each other, their mirrored features creating an almost surreal tableau. Eustace remained silent, his keen eyes observing every flicker of emotion, every subtle movement.

This was the moment he had orchestrated, the collision of two lives that seemed inexplicably intertwined. Whatever secrets lay between them, he was determined to uncover them—for Clara's sake, and for his own.

The air between them felt impossibly heavy, charged with something she couldn't name. Her trembling voice broke the silence. "This feels like a sick kind of joke."

The words came out sharper than she intended, her shock crackling through her tone. Her eyes darted between Eustace and the woman in front of her—the woman who *was* her, and yet wasn't.

Vittoria didn't answer immediately. She stood rooted to the spot, her lips parting slightly as though she'd forgotten how to speak. Her porcelain composure cracked, her wide blue eyes scanning Clara's face with an intensity that bordered on disbelief.

"You..." Vittoria finally managed, her voice soft and unsteady. "You look exactly like me."

The unguarded shock in her voice caught Clara off guard, sending an odd pang through her chest.

"This—" Clara took a step back, her head shaking as her pulse hammered in her ears. "I know you've explained this before, but it is ridiculous. Who are you?"

Vittoria mirrored her step back, her hand lifting instinctively to her chest. "Who am I? Who are you?"

"That's Vittoria," Eustace cut in, his tone unusually cautious. "And Clara, she's—"

"Stop," Clara snapped, the words louder than she'd intended. Her mind felt like it was splintering. "I know who she is. Everyone thinks I'm her. That's the whole problem!" She gestured wildly between them, the hysteria bubbling up in her voice. "But why does she look like *me*?"

Vittoria blinked, her face pale. "I... I don't know." Her voice cracked slightly, losing its polished edge. Her gaze darted to Eustace, then back to Clara. "This isn't... I wasn't prepared for this."

"Well, neither was I!" Clara shot back, her panic overtaking her usual self-control.

The silence stretched, thick and suffocating, broken only by Clara's ragged breathing. Vittoria's hands twisted together as she stared, seemingly at a loss for words.

Eustace cleared his throat, his voice low but deliberate. "Perhaps you two should sit down."

Neither of them moved. Clara's legs felt too shaky, and Vittoria looked as though she'd been struck by lightning.

"I don't..." Vittoria began again, her voice faint. "I don't understand how this is possible."

Clara swallowed hard, trying to steady herself. "Neither do I," she admitted, her tone quieter now, though the tremor hadn't left her voice. Her gaze darted to Eustace, her brow furrowing. "Did you know about this?"

He hesitated, his face unreadable. "I suspected there was a connection. But this..." He gestured vaguely between them. "I knew, but it's still very shocking to see the resemblance."

Vittoria's trembling hand reached out slightly, then dropped back to her side as though unsure of what to do. "This can't be a coincidence," she murmured, more to herself than anyone else.

Clara let out a hollow laugh, though it carried no humor. "You think?" She pressed a hand to her temple, trying to calm the storm of questions raging in her mind.

"Actually, I think I know what this is."

Clara's gaze snapped to Eustace, then back to the woman in front of her. Vittoria nodded, her expression softening.

"I had a twin sister," Vittoria began, her voice steady but laced with emotion. "Or rather... I heard I had one. I remember little of her." She paused, and her hands twisted together in a rare display of nervousness. "She was taken from us when I was very young. My father looked for her for years, but he never found her."

The words hit Clara like a physical blow. Her knees felt weak, and she stumbled back into the nearest chair, gripping the armrest as if it might anchor her.

"No," she whispered, shaking her head. "That can't be true."

"It is," Vittoria said, stepping closer.

Clara couldn't think, couldn't breathe. Her mind raced with memories she'd buried long ago—fleeting images of faces she didn't recognize, whispers of dreams that felt too real.

"No," she said again, her voice firmer this time. "You've got it wrong. My parents... They—"

Her words faltered. She thought of her father, his cruelty, the way he sneered every time she tried to ask questions about her childhood. She thought of her mother, a woman who had loved her but never offered explanations for why they had so little, why there were no family portraits, no stories about a happier past.

Her chest tightened, and she pressed a hand to it, trying to steady her breathing.

"You have the same birthmark," Eustace said quietly, his tone soothing but insistent.

The tension in the room was unbearable, stretching between them like a taut thread ready to snap. Clara's breathing was shallow, her heart racing so fast it felt as though it might burst from her chest. Vittoria mirrored her unease, her usually composed demeanor shattered into raw, uncertain pieces.

The silence broke when Vittoria's gaze fell to Clara's hand, her expression flickering with something between recognition and disbelief. "Your hand," she whispered, her voice trembling.

Clara followed her gaze, frowning. "What about it?"

"The mark," Vittoria said, stepping closer now despite visible hesitation. "Do you have one? Here." She held up her own hand, gesturing to her pinky finger.

Clara's frown deepened, but she lifted her hand slowly, unwillingly. Her breath caught when she saw the tiny crescent-shaped mark on Vittoria's finger—an exact match to the one she'd always had but never thought twice about.

Her voice came out hoarse. "That doesn't prove anything."

Vittoria didn't respond. Her eyes were wide, almost glassy, as though she'd seen a ghost. She whispered softly, almost too quietly for Clara to hear, "It's impossible."

"What's impossible?" Clara demanded, her voice shaking.

"Everything... that you are alive even though we searched the whole world for you, but somehow you've lived unnoticed up to this time. It is a miracle."

"No," she whispered, her head shaking. "No, it just doesn't make any sense."

Vittoria's voice grew softer, almost pleading. "It does. Look at us. The birthmark, our faces..." She trailed off, her words hanging in the air.

Clara's mind reeled, memories she'd long buried surfacing like ghosts. Her father's mocking laughter, her mother's vague answers about the past, the strange dreams she'd always dismissed—dreams of warmth, of laughter, of holding another hand in hers.

"No," she said again, her voice louder this time, more desperate. "I'm not some long-lost twin. I'm just a seamstress."

"You're more than that," Vittoria said softly, her eyes glistening with unshed tears.

Clara's chest ached as the truth she didn't want to face began to settle over her. Her fingers reached for the locket around her neck, the one she'd always clung to but never questioned. She pulled it out slowly, her trembling hands cradling the small gold pendant as though it might hold the answers she so desperately needed.

When Vittoria gasped, Clara's heart dropped.

"You have one too," Vittoria whispered, her voice breaking.

Clara's eyes darted to the identical chain resting against Vittoria's gown. The matching lockets shone in the dim light, two halves of a whole.

"This..." Clara's voice cracked. "This doesn't mean anything."

"It means everything," Vittoria said, stepping closer again. Her voice was trembling now, her calm composure completely gone. "They were made for us. I've had mine my whole life. You must have had yours too."

Clara shook her head, tears streaming down her face. "This can't be real."

"It is," Vittoria said firmly, though her own tears had begun to fall. "It has to be. I remember... I remember you."

The room spun around Clara as Vittoria's words hit her like a tidal wave. "No," she whispered, barely able to speak. "You're wrong."

"I'm not," Vittoria said, her voice breaking. "I remember holding your hand in the nursery. I remember the way you used to laugh when our governess sang. I remember you."

Clara's hands trembled as she clutched the locket tightly, her tears falling harder now. The memories Vittoria described felt like distant echoes, fragments she'd always thought were dreams.

Her voice was barely audible. "I don't know who I am anymore."

\*\*\*

The room blurred as Clara gripped the locket tighter, her breath hitching as tears streamed freely down her cheeks. Vittoria's words swirled in her mind—hand-holding in the nursery, laughter, songs. Distant images flickered in her memory like the faint glow of a candle barely clinging to life.

A soft melody echoed in her head, a woman's voice humming a lullaby she'd long forgotten. She had always thought it was something she'd imagined, a figment of her childhood mind filling the silence of long nights. But now it felt real. Too real.

Clara stumbled back, clutching the back of the chair for support. Her legs felt weak, and the walls seemed to close in around her. Every piece of her carefully constructed identity was falling apart.

She didn't belong anywhere—not here, not with the nobility, and not in the life she had built as a seamstress. She didn't even know who she was anymore.

"Clara."

Her name sounded foreign on Vittoria's lips. She couldn't bear to hear it right now. She shook her head, her voice trembling. "I need to leave."

Vittoria stepped forward, concern clouding her features. "Wait—"

"No," Clara snapped, surprising even herself. Her tears blurred her vision as she turned to Eustace, whose gaze burned into hers, steady and unreadable. "Take me home. Please."

His jaw tightened, but he nodded. "Of course."

She didn't remember much of the journey back to Ravencroft House. The carriage rocked gently, but Clara barely felt it. Her thoughts were too loud, the questions and memories tangling in a mess she couldn't untangle. Eustace sat across from her, silent but watching. Always watching.

*** 

The moment Clara stepped into her room, she let the mask drop. The weight of the locket in her hand felt unbearable. She ripped it from her neck and flung it onto the desk as though it burned her.

She paced the small space, her movements frantic. Her skirts swished against the floor as she dragged her hands through her hair, pulling at the pins until the strands tumbled free.

Flashes of memories came unbidden, each one sharper than the last.

A tiny room bathed in sunlight, the smell of fresh lavender in the air. A little hand clasping hers, tugging her toward a window. A deep voice murmuring promises of safety. The scream of a woman, distant but echoing in her ears.

"No," she whispered, pressing her palms to her temples. The room spun again, and she sank onto the bed, her breathing ragged.

Her mother's face came into focus—not the woman she knows as mother now, but the one from her faintest memories. Gentle hands brushing through her hair, a locket being fastened around her neck. "This will always remind you of where you belong," her mother's voice whispered in her mind.

Clara's chest tightened painfully. Had her family known? Who were they really? Had they stolen her away? The questions burned through her, each one heavier than the last.

---

The soft knock at her door startled her. She wiped at her cheeks hastily, though she doubted it would fool anyone.

"Clara?"

Eustace's voice sent a fresh wave of emotion crashing over her. She didn't respond, but the door creaked open anyway.

He stepped inside, his presence filling the room like it always did. She hated how much comfort she felt at the sight of him, how his steady gaze seemed to anchor her even when she was falling apart.

"Go away," she mumbled, turning her back to him.

"No." His tone left no room for argument.

She heard the soft scrape of a chair being pulled closer, then felt the weight of his gaze on her back. "You're not running from this."

"I'm not running," she snapped, though it felt like a lie even as she said it.

"You're not running," he repeated, his voice quieter now. "But you're breaking."

The words hit her harder than she expected. Her shoulders trembled, and she hugged herself tighter, her nails digging into her arms.

"Let me help," he said.

Her laugh was bitter. "Help? How could you possibly help? You don't even know who I am."

"I know enough."

She spun to face him, her eyes blazing. "You know nothing. I'm not Vittoria. I'm not anyone. I don't belong here. I don't belong anywhere!"

Eustace didn't flinch. His expression was calm but fierce, his gaze locked onto hers as though he could will her to believe him. "You belong with me."

The words knocked the breath out of her. She stared at him, her chest heaving as she tried to process what he was saying.

"Eustace—"

"I don't care about names, or titles, or birthmarks," he said, rising to his feet. His hands clenched at his sides, his frustration barely contained. "I care about you, Clara. The woman who fights for herself. The woman who doesn't back down from a challenge. The woman who has somehow managed to turn my entire life upside down."

Tears welled in her eyes again, but she bit her lip, trying to hold them back. "I'm scared," she admitted, her voice breaking.

"I know," he said softly, his tone losing its edge. He stepped closer, his movements slow and deliberate. "But you're not alone. Not anymore."

Clara's resolve crumbled. The tears spilled over, and she covered her face with her hands. Eustace closed the distance between them, his arms wrapping around her with a firmness that felt like a promise.

"Stay," he murmured into her hair. "Stay with me."

She shook her head against his chest. "My stepfamily—"

"I'll take care of them," he said without hesitation.

"You can't promise that."

"Yes, I can."

His voice was so certain, so unwavering, that for a moment she believed him. She pulled back slightly, her tear-streaked face tilting up to meet his gaze.

"Why?" she asked, her voice trembling. "Why would you do this for me?"

He cupped her face gently, his thumb brushing away a tear. "Because I can't imagine a life without you in it."

The raw sincerity in his voice broke something in her. She surged upward, her lips finding his in a kiss that was both desperate and filled with every unspoken emotion she couldn't put into words.

When they finally broke apart, her heart was racing, her breathing uneven. But for the first time, she felt a flicker of hope.

"I'll stay," she whispered. "But only if you promise me one thing."

"Anything."

She met his gaze, her own steady now. "Promise me you won't let me lose myself again."

Eustace's grip tightened slightly, and he nodded. "I promise."

# Chapter Sixteen

Eustace stood at the edge of the huge ballroom, his dark gaze fixed on Clara as she twirled across the floor with one of his younger cousins who happened to be in town.

The sight of her—radiant in a gown of deep burgundy silk that he now knew she'd made herself—stirred something fierce in his chest.

She was everything he'd never known he wanted.

Everything he now couldn't imagine living without.

*Since when did she become so important to him?*

"Your Grace?" Lady Pembroke, one of the suitor-hungry mama's voices cut through his thoughts. "You seem rather distracted this evening."

Eustace barely spared her a glance. "Do I?"

"Quite." The older woman's tone carried a hint of amusement. "Though I can hardly blame you. The countess looks particularly lovely tonight."

*The countess.*

His jaw tightened at the reminder of their precarious situation. Even now, after discovering Clara's true identity as Vittoria's long-lost twin, the ton still believed her to be the countess herself.

He didn't know what to do about that yet or how to maneuver the situation, because the truth would definitely come out soon enough, but for now...

"Indeed she does," he replied curtly, his attention drawn back to Clara as the dance ended.

She made her way toward him, her cheeks flushed from exertion and her eyes bright with joy.

Something in his chest constricted at the sight. How had he ever thought he could maintain a false engagement with this woman without losing his heart in the process?

"My Lord Duke," she said as she reached him, dropping into a playful curtsey. "Are you planning to lurk in corners all evening?"

"I do not lurk," he corrected, though his lips twitched. "I observe."

"Oh? And what do you observe?"

He stepped closer, lowering his voice so only she could hear. "I observe that you've danced with every gentleman except me."

Clara's eyes sparkled with mischief. "Perhaps because you haven't asked?"

"A grievous oversight." He extended his hand just as the opening notes of a waltz filled the air. "Would you do me the honor, beautiful lady?"

She placed her hand in his, and the familiar warmth of her touch sent a jolt through him. As he led her onto the floor, he couldn't help but remember their first dance at the masquerade ball—when he'd thought her someone else entirely. How blind he'd been then.

"You're thinking very loudly," Clara murmured as they began to move.

Eustace drew her slightly closer than was strictly proper, savoring the way she fit perfectly in his arms. "I'm thinking about how different things were at our first ball."

"Ah." A shadow crossed her face. "When you thought I was Vittoria."

"When I was a fool," he corrected, guiding her through a turn. "I didn't see what was right in front of me."

Her expression softened. "And what do you see now?"

"I see you, Clara." His voice dropped lower, rougher. "Only you."

The vulnerability that flashed across her face made him want to sweep her away from the crowded ballroom, away from prying eyes and wagging tongues. But he couldn't. Not yet.

They moved together in perfect synchronization, as they had since that very first night. Other couples swirled around them, but Eustace barely noticed. His world had narrowed to the woman in his arms—to the subtle scent of lavender that always clung to her skin, to the way her hand gripped his just a fraction tighter when he guided her through a complicated turn.

"Everyone is staring," she whispered, though her steps never faltered.

"Let them." His thumb traced a small circle on her lower back. "You're worth staring at."

A becoming blush colored her cheeks. "Careful, Your Grace. One might think you're becoming romantic."

"Heaven forbid." But there was no heat in his words, only a warmth that seemed reserved solely for her.

As the music drew to a close, Eustace found himself reluctant to let her go. The evening felt charged somehow, as though they were balanced on the edge of something momentous. He'd learned to trust his instincts over the years, and right now, they were screaming at him to keep Clara close.

"Would you like some air?" he asked, noting the flush in her cheeks.

She nodded, and he guided her toward the terrace doors, his hand settling possessively at the small of her back. Let the ton gossip about that if they wished. Soon enough, they'd have far more interesting things to discuss.

\*\*\*

And sure enough, the night air had barely cooled Clara's flushed cheeks when the first ripple of disturbance reached them. A hush fell over the ballroom behind them, the kind of sudden silence that spoke of impending disaster.

Eustace felt it before he saw it—a shift in the atmosphere that made his spine stiffen. Years of navigating society's treacherous waters had honed his instincts, and right now, every one of them screamed danger.

"Your Grace!" A breathless footman appeared at the terrace door. "Lord Edmund Blackthorne has—"

But the rest of his warning was cut short as Edmund's voice boomed through the ballroom, carrying clearly to where they stood.

"Ladies and gentlemen of the ton!" The sound made Clara freeze beside him. "I apologize for interrupting this lovely evening, but I bring news that cannot wait."

Eustace's hand tightened on Clara's waist as he turned them both to face the scene unfolding inside. Edmund stood at the top of the grand staircase, commanding attention like an actor on a stage. In his hands, he clutched a leather portfolio that made Clara's breath hitch.

"What is it?" Eustace murmured, noting her reaction.

"Those are—" She swallowed hard. "Those look like my ledgers. From my shop."

Ice slid down Eustace's spine. *Dear God.*

"For months now," Edmund continued, his voice dripping with false regret, "we have all been deceived by an imposter in our midst. A woman who has played us for fools, who has lied her way into our highest circles, and who even now attempts to corrupt one of our most noble families through deception and fraud."

Whispers erupted through the crowd. Dozens of heads looked around, unsure what was going on.

"My Lord Edmund," Lady Hartley stepped forward, her voice sharp. "This is hardly the time or place—"

"Oh, but it is exactly the time and place." Edmund's smile was cruel as he began descending the stairs. "When better to expose a fraud than when she stands to lose everything? When the entire ton can witness the truth about the woman who dares to call herself Countess Vittoria Romano?"

All heads turned sharply toward the terrace where Eustace and Clara stood. He could feel her trembling against him.

"I have here," Edmund held up the portfolio, "proof that your beloved countess is nothing more than a common seamstress. A girl from the gutters who has orchestrated the most audacious fraud in recent memory."

He pulled out a stack of papers, letting them flutter down the stairs. "Receipts from her shop in Cheapside. Letters from clients who knew her as Madame Celestine. Testimony from her neighbors about her common birth and upbringing."

Each word fell like a hammer blow. Eustace could feel Clara's reputation—her entire world—crumbling around them with every damning piece of evidence.

"But perhaps most incriminating of all," Edmund's voice turned silky with triumph, "is this letter from her own father, detailing exactly how she plotted to infiltrate our society by impersonating the real Countess Vittoria."

The shock in the room was palpable. Ladies clutched their fans, gentlemen muttered in outrage, and all eyes fixed on Clara with a mixture of horror and fascination.

"She has made fools of us all," Edmund declared. "But most especially of you, Your Grace." His gaze fixed on Eustace with mock sympathy. "To think, the Duke of Ravencroft, nearly trapped into marriage with a common thief and liar."

Eustace felt something dark and dangerous rise in his chest—a fury he hadn't felt in years. But before he could speak, Clara's grip on his arm loosened.

She stepped forward, her head high despite the tears that threatened to fall. The movement drew every eye in the room.

"Clara," Eustace growled, reaching for her. "Don't—"

But she was already walking toward Edmund, each step measured and deliberate. The crowd parted before her like water, their judgment hanging heavy in the air.

Edmund's smile widened as she approached, triumph gleaming in his eyes. He clearly thought he'd won.

But Eustace knew better. He'd seen that look in Clara's eyes before—the same fire that had first drawn him to her, the strength that had made him fall in love with her.

She wasn't backing down.

She was preparing for war.

The entire ballroom held its breath, waiting to see what would happen next. In that moment, Eustace realized that everything—their reputation, their future, their very lives in society—balanced on what happened in the next few minutes.

And somewhere in the back of his mind, he wondered if Edmund had any idea what he'd just started.

Clara stood before Edmund, her burgundy skirts settling around her like a queen's robes. The silence in the ballroom was absolute, broken only by the rustle of silk as the ton leaned forward, eager to witness her downfall.

"Are you quite finished, my lord?" Her voice carried clearly, steadier than Eustace had expected.

Edmund's smile faltered slightly. "I beg your pardon?"

"I asked if you were finished." She gestured to the scattered papers on the stairs. "With your theatrical performance."

A low murmur rippled through the crowd. Eustace moved closer, ready to intervene, but something in Clara's stance made him pause.

"This is no performance, madam." Edmund spat the word like poison. "These are facts. Evidence of your deception. Will you deny that you are Clara Mills, a common seamstress?"

Clara lifted her chin. "I am Clara Mills."

The admission sent shockwaves through the room. Ladies gasped, fans fluttering frantically as they whispered behind them. But Clara wasn't finished.

"I am Clara Mills," she repeated, her voice growing stronger. "And I am also Madame Celestine, the modiste who has dressed half the ladies in this room." Her gaze swept the crowd, landing pointedly on several women who suddenly looked uncomfortable. "Including your own sister, Lord Edmund, who praised my work just last week."

Edmund's face reddened. "You admit to your fraud then?"

"What I admit to," Clara said, taking another step forward, "is surviving. What I admit to is using the talents I was given to make my way in the world. But fraud?" She shook her head. "No, my lord. That accusation comes too late."

Eustace chose that moment to move. He strode forward, his presence commanding immediate attention as he took his place beside Clara.

"Too late," he repeated, his voice carrying the full weight of his authority, "because what Lord Edmund fails to mention is that we have already uncovered the actual truth, not some fabricated story."

But before Edmund could respond with another cutting remark, the ballroom doors swung open once more.

"Yes, this female is Clara Mills, but she is also my sister."

The voice—so familiar yet different—cut through the tension like a blade. The crowd parted, revealing a figure that drew collective gasps of shock from the assembled ton.

Countess Vittoria Romano stood in the doorway, resplendent in deep blue silk that perfectly matched the gown she'd worn the night of her own debut years ago. The resemblance between her and Clara was extraordinary—like looking into a mirror with the subtlest of changes. Where Clara's chin tilted in defiance, Vittoria's lifted with aristocratic grace. Where Clara's eyes blazed with hard-won strength, Vittoria's held the quiet confidence of one born to power.

Edmund's face drained of color. "But—but you're in Italy. You can't be—"

"I assure you, Lord Edmund, I am quite real." Vittoria's voice carried the crystalline perfection of her noble upbringing as she glided forward. "Though I must say, your treatment of my sister leaves much to be desired."

She reached Clara's side, taking her hand. The sight of them together struck the room silent—there could be no denying the truth of their connection now.

"Sister?" Lady Pembrooke's voice quavered from the crowd.

"Yes," Vittoria confirmed, her grip on Clara's hand tightening. "But I shall explain that later, for now there's something else everyone must know."

Eustace watched as tears spilled down Clara's cheeks, matched by the glimmer in Vittoria's eyes. The sisters stood together, united against the world that had kept them apart for so long.

"But how—" Edmund started, his carefully crafted exposure crumbling around him.

"How?" Vittoria's laugh held a sharp edge. "Perhaps you should ask the man who stole her."

The doors to the ballroom burst open. A commotion near the entrance drew all eyes as several of Eustace's most trusted men escorted a struggling figure into the room.

Clara's stepfather, Richard Mills, looked considerably less impressive than usual—his clothes disheveled, his face marked with the stubble of several days in custody.

"What is the meaning of this?" Edmund demanded, but there was a note of uncertainty in his voice now.

Eustace's smile was cold. "Mr. Mills, perhaps you'd like to share with the assembled company exactly how you came to raise Clara Mills as your stepdaughter?"

The man's face went pale. "I—I don't—"

"Or shall I tell them?" Eustace continued relentlessly. "About how you were hired by a rival family to kidnap one of the Romano twins? About how you stole a child from that family and smuggled her to England?"

"Paid handsomely by Lord Edmund's father to steal a young child from the Romano family nearly two decades ago."

A collective gasp rippled through the ballroom, as scandalous whispers filled the air. Clara's breath hitched; her eyes wide as she turned toward Eustace. He gave her a small, reassuring nod before stepping forward, his voice steady and unyielding.

"You see," Eustace addressed the crowd, "this isn't merely a case of mistaken identity or fraud. This is a deliberate conspiracy—a crime committed to destabilize one of the most prominent families in Europe. Clara Mills was never meant to grow up in obscurity. She is the rightful twin of Countess Vittoria Romano."

The room erupted in shocked murmurs, but Eustace wasn't finished.

"Mr. Mills," he continued, his gaze piercing, "was recruited by none other than the Blackthorne family to ensure that Vittoria's twin would vanish. Why? Because they sought to weaken the Romano family by creating discord in their succession line. A single heir is vulnerable, after all. With one sister missing, the family's enemies hoped to exploit that weakness, gaining power and influence over their trade empire."

Edmund's face turned ashen. "This is preposterous!" he barked, though his voice lacked its usual confidence.

Eustace ignored him, addressing the crowd instead. "The evidence is clear. Clara's stepfather confessed everything to my men when confronted with proof of his payments—payments that originated from Lord Blackthorne's own accounts. And now that the true heir has been reunited with her family, the truth can no longer be hidden."

Clara's stepfather, now shaking visibly, tried to stammer out a denial, but Vittoria silenced him with a cold glare. "Enough lies, Mr. Mills. You've caused enough damage to my family—and to my sister."

Clara's voice, quiet but firm, cut through the noise. "So my whole life was a lie?" She turned to Eustace, her eyes brimming with tears. "Everything I've ever known—"

Gasps echoed through the ballroom. Clara's hands trembled.

Richard Mills seemed to collapse in on himself. "It wasn't—I never meant—"

"Oh, but you did," Eustace cut in. "And now you'll face the consequences of your actions." He turned to address the stunned crowd. "Ladies and gentlemen, he took Clara's hand, lifting it to press a kiss to her knuckles. "The woman before you is not Countess Vittoria Romano. She is Lady Clara Romano, the long-lost twin sister of the countess, stolen from her family as a child and only now restored to her rightful place."

The revelation hit the room like a thunderclap. Edmund staggered back, his carefully orchestrated exposure crumbling around him.

"Impossible," he whispered.

"I assure you, it is quite possible." Eustace's voice hardened. "We have proof of her birth, testimony from the countess herself, and now..." He gestured to Richard Mills. "A confession from one of the perpetrators."

Clara stood tall beside him, her fingers interlaced with his. "I may not have been raised as a noblewoman," she said, addressing the room at large, "but I am proud of who I am. Of what I've accomplished. And I will not apologize for surviving."

The tide of opinion in the room was shifting; Eustace could feel it. Where there had been scandal and condemnation, now there was fascination and even admiration. The ton loved nothing more than a dramatic revelation, and this was better than anything they could have imagined.

"Furthermore," Eustace added, his voice carrying an edge of steel, "any who wish to question Lady Clara's place in society will answer to me. Not as her fiancé, but as her champion."

Edmund's final attempt at dignity crumbled. "Your Grace, I... I had no idea—"

"No," Eustace agreed coldly. "You didn't. You were so eager to destroy what you didn't understand that you never bothered to look deeper. That will be your legacy, Edmund. Remember it well."

# Chapter Seventeen

Clara stood in the center of the ballroom, her heart thundering against her ribs as the whispers died down around her.

Everything was out now—every secret, every lie, every truth she'd been too afraid to face. The revelation of her true identity still hung like scattered diamonds, catching the light and reflecting it back tenfold.

She couldn't quite believe it. After so many years of hiding, of pretending, of being afraid... here she was.

*Just Clara.*

Finally, completely herself.

A hysterical little laugh bubbled up in her throat. Lord Edmund's face had been priceless when Vittoria had stepped forward. And her stepfather—that horrible, cruel man—was being led away in chains. It felt like a dream.

But it wasn't a dream. This was real.

Her fingers smoothed down the front of her gown—one of her own creations, of course. Every stitch, every careful detail had been crafted by her own hands. The deep blue silk whispered against the floor as she took a step forward, then another.

"Well," she muttered under her breath, unable to help herself, "at least now they know why their dresses fit so perfectly."

She caught a few ladies examining their own gowns with new eyes, and another laugh threatened to escape. The whole thing was rather ridiculous when she thought about it. All that fuss about bloodlines and titles, and here she was—both a seamstress and a noble lady.

The ballroom seemed to hold its breath, waiting to see what she would do next. Clara lifted her chin, feeling strangely light. For the first time in her life, she didn't have to pretend. Didn't have to watch her words or guard her expressions or try to be someone else.

She was just... free.

"Ladies and gentlemen," she said, her voice carrying across the silent room with surprising strength. "I believe proper introductions are in order."

A few people shifted uncomfortably, but most remained frozen, watching her with a mixture of shock and fascination. Clara felt a smile tugging at her lips—not the demure one she'd practiced in mirrors, but her real smile. The one that always made her stepfather say she was too bold.

"My name is Clara Mills... Romano now. Yes, I am Lady Vittoria's twin sister, lost as a child and raised without knowledge of my true heritage." She paused, letting that sink in before continuing. "But I am also Madame Celestine, the seamstress who has dressed half of you this season."

More whispers erupted, and she saw several women clutching at their gowns. Lady Pembroke, wearing one of Clara's finest creations, actually squeaked.

"Oh yes," Clara couldn't resist adding, her natural sass creeping into her voice. "That exquisite ball gown you're wearing, Lady Pembroke? Every stitch was placed by these supposedly common hands."

She held up her hands, showing the tiny calluses and pinpricks that no amount of careful grooming could hide. Marks of her craft, her passion—and she was no longer ashamed of them.

"I've spent years hiding who I am, trying to be what others wanted me to be. But I'm done with that." Her voice grew stronger, filling the vast room. "I am a noblewoman by birth, yes. But I am also a seamstress by choice and talent. Both are part of who I am, and I won't apologize for either."

She turned slowly, meeting the eyes of those around her. Some looked away, but others—more than she expected—held her gaze with something like respect.

"To those who have worn my creations —thank you for trusting in my skill, even if you didn't know it was mine. To those who thought they knew me as Vittoria—I apologize for the deception, but I hope you can understand why it was necessary."

The silence that followed was different now—less shocked, more contemplative. Clara felt something settle in her chest, a certainty she'd never known before. This was who she was meant to be—not just a noble lady, not just a talented seamstress, but both. All of it. Everything.

She was Clara Romano, and she would never hide again.

Clara felt lighter than she had in years, the truth finally spoken aloud. But her stepbrother Thomas wasn't about to let her have this moment. His voice cut through the contemplative silence like a rusty blade.

"How dare you claim such a title?" He shouldered his way through the crowd, his face mottled with rage. "You're nothing but a common seamstress who got lucky. A pretender who—"

"Oh, do shut up, Thomas." Clara didn't even bother turning to face him. She'd spent too many years cowering from that voice. "Your father's just been arrested for kidnapping me as a child. I don't think you're in any position to talk about pretending."

A few shocked laughs rippled through the crowd. Thomas spluttered, his face turning an interesting shade of purple that clashed horribly with his cravat. Clara noted absently that she could have done a much better job with that particular piece of neckwear.

"You can't speak to me like that!" he hissed. "You're just a—"

"A what?" Now she did turn, fixing him with the look she usually reserved for particularly difficult customers who couldn't make up their minds about fabric choices. "A seamstress? Yes, we've established that. A noblewoman? Also true, as my sister Vittoria has so kindly confirmed. So which part exactly are you objecting to?"

Her stepbrother took a menacing step forward, but Clara didn't flinch. She'd spent too many years flinching.

"You think these people will accept you?" He gestured wildly at the assembled crowd. "Half of them are wearing your dresses—do you think they'll ever forgive that humiliation?"

Clara couldn't help it—she laughed. The sound echoed off the high ceiling, genuine and free. "Humiliation? Thomas, darling, do you know how much they paid for these dresses? How many of them begged for appointments with Madame Celestine?"

She turned to the crowd, spreading her arms. "Ladies, I ask you—are you humiliated by wearing a dress that fits perfectly? That makes you feel beautiful? That turns heads when you enter a room?"

She paused, her eyes twinkling. "Or are you perhaps more humiliated by standing next to someone wearing an obviously poorly tied cravat?"

This time the laughter was louder, less restrained. She saw several ladies hiding smiles behind their fans, and more than a few gentlemen adjusting their own neckwear self-consciously.

"You little—" Thomas started forward but froze as Vittoria stepped up beside Clara.

"I wouldn't finish that sentence if I were you," Vittoria said, her voice cool and refined but carrying an edge sharp enough to cut. "That's my sister you're speaking to."

Clara felt warmth bloom in her chest at those words. Sister. It still felt surreal, but right. Like a dress that had been perfectly fitted all along, just waiting to be worn.

"Besides," Clara added, unable to resist, "if you're so concerned about humiliation, perhaps you should consider that you're currently making a scene at a ball hosted by the Duke of Ravencroft. Not very gentlemanly behavior, wouldn't you say?"

Thomas' mouth opened and closed several times, but no sound came out. He looked around wildly, seemingly just realizing that every eye in the room was on him—and not in the way he would have wished.

"I suggest," Clara said, her voice honey-sweet but her eyes sharp, "that you follow your father's example and make a quick exit. Though preferably without the chains—they're so last season."

The titters that followed her words were the final blow. Thomas backed away, his face now an alarming shade of puce, before turning and practically running from the ballroom.

Clara watched him go, feeling oddly peaceful. How strange that the same man who had terrorized her for years now seemed so... small.

"Well," she said to no one in particular, "I suppose that's one way to liven up a ball."

Clara caught Eustace's gaze a few feet beside her and nearly lost her breath. He was staring at her with such naked pride, such fierce admiration that it made her cheeks warm. His dark eyes hadn't left her once during her confrontation with Thomas, and now they held something that made her heart skip—something that looked remarkably like love.

But before she could dwell on that particular revelation, movement from the corner of her eye caught her attention. Her breath hitched as she saw Eustace's mother and sister making their way toward her.

Oh lord. This was it.

Lady Margaret reached her first, practically bouncing with each step. Clara braced herself, but nothing could have prepared her for Margaret throwing her arms around her in a very unladylike embrace.

"I knew it!" Margaret exclaimed, squeezing Clara tight. "I knew there was something special about you. No wonder you were so talented with my dresses!"

Clara stood frozen for a moment, her arms awkwardly at her sides before slowly returning the hug. Over Margaret's shoulder, she saw the Dowager Duchess approaching more sedately, her expression unreadable.

Her stomach twisted. This was the woman whose son she had deceived, whose household she had infiltrated under false pretenses. If anyone had the right to be angry...

"Your Grace," Clara started, disentangling herself from Margaret. "I—"

"My dear," the Dowager interrupted, her voice gentler than Clara had ever heard it, "I believe under the circumstances you should call me Mother."

Clara's mouth fell open. Across the room, she saw Eustace's lips twitch into a smile, his eyes dancing with amusement at her obvious shock.

"But..." Clara struggled to find words. "I deceived you. I pretended to be someone else. I—"

"You brought life back to this house," the Dowager said firmly. "You made my son smile again. You showed kindness to every servant, patience with my daughter's endless fashion queries, and demonstrated more grace under pressure than most born to it." She paused, her eyes softening. "And if I'm not mistaken, you've managed to do what no one else could—make my son fall in love."

Clara's face flamed as her gaze automatically sought Eustace again. He was still watching her, looking utterly unrepentant about it. In fact, he seemed to be enjoying her flustered state entirely too much.

"Besides," Margaret added cheerfully, "now I'll never have to worry about my dresses again. I'll have the most talented modiste in London right in the family!"

"Margaret!" the Dowager chided, but her lips were twitching.

Clara couldn't help it—she laughed, the sound bubbling up from somewhere deep inside her. It was ridiculous and perfect and everything she'd never dared to hope for.

"I'd be honored," she managed, her voice thick with emotion, "to call you Mother."

The Dowager's eyes sparkled suspiciously as she pulled Clara into a proper embrace. Over her shoulder, Clara saw Vittoria watching with a soft smile, and beyond her, Eustace had moved closer, his presence drawing eyes from around the room.

He looked resplendent in his evening clothes, every inch the powerful duke he was, but his eyes were soft as they rested on her. The way he was looking at her made her feel like the most precious thing in the room, titles and talents aside.

She'd spent so long being afraid of being discovered, of being rejected. But here she was, surrounded by people who accepted her—all of her. The seamstress and the noble lady. The lost child and the found sister. The woman who had finally, finally found where she belonged.

Clara felt Eustace's hand settle on her waist before she registered his presence beside her. He'd moved so quietly, but now he was there, solid and warm, his thumb tracing small circles against her side. The gesture was subtle enough to be proper, yet intimate enough to make her pulse flutter.

Vittoria approached them, her eyes bright with unshed tears. "I've written to Father and Mother," she said softly.

Clara's breath caught. Parents. Real parents. Not her stepfather with his cruel smiles and grasping hands, but the ones she barely remembered—just fragments of warm embraces and gentle voices.

"They never stopped looking for you," Vittoria continued, reaching for Clara's hands. "Mother will be beside herself. She's kept your nursery exactly as it was, you know. Wouldn't let anyone change a thing."

Eustace's arm tightened around Clara's waist as she swayed slightly. He was so close now she could feel his breath stirring her hair, grounding her as emotions threatened to overwhelm her.

"What are they like?" Clara whispered, squeezing Vittoria's hands. "Our parents?"

Vittoria's face lit up. "Father is... well, he's rather like you actually. Stubborn as a mule and too clever by half." Her eyes danced with amusement. "He'll adore that you've made something of yourself. He's always saying that nobility without purpose is just decoration."

Clara felt Eustace's quiet chuckle rumble through her back. "That explains a few things," he murmured, his lips close to her ear.

"And Mother," Vittoria continued, either not noticing or politely ignoring their closeness, "she's the kindest person you'll ever meet. But don't let that fool you—she runs the estate with an iron fist in a velvet glove."

"She sounds wonderful," Clara managed, her voice thick.

"She is. And she's been keeping a journal for you, you know. Every day since you were taken. Writing down everything she wished she could tell you, everything she hoped you'd know someday."

The tears Clara had been holding back spilled over. Eustace's free hand found hers, their fingers intertwining as Vittoria stepped closer, completing their little circle.

"I know it's overwhelming," Vittoria said gently. "But you're not alone anymore, Clara. You have a family—a real one."

"I have two," Clara corrected, glancing between her sister and Eustace. His dark eyes met hers, full of promises she was finally ready to believe in.

"Speaking of family," Vittoria said, a mischievous glint entering her eye, "Mother will be thrilled about Eustace. She always said it was fate that broke our original engagement."

Clara felt Eustace stiffen slightly behind her. "Did she now?"

"Oh yes." Vittoria's smile widened. "She said the stars must have known you were meant for my sister instead."

Clara turned to look up at Eustace, finding his gaze already on her. The love in his eyes was unmistakable now, unguarded and pure. The whole ballroom seemed to fade away, leaving just this—just them.

"Your mother sounds very wise," he said softly, his words meant only for Clara.

"Speaking of which," Vittoria said, taking a deliberate step back, her smile knowing, "I believe you had something you wanted to say to my sister, Your Grace?"

Clara frowned at Vittoria's retreating back, then turned to Eustace. "What is she talking about?"

But the words died in her throat. Eustace had shifted to face her fully, and something in his expression made her heart stutter. His dark eyes held hers with an intensity that made the rest of the ballroom fade away.

"Clara," he said, his voice low but carrying in the sudden hush that had fallen over the room. "My impossible, brilliant Clara."

She felt her cheeks warm. "Eustace—"

"No," he interrupted gently. "Let me say this. I've been watching you tonight—watching you stand up to your stepbrother, claim your identity, face down every challenge with that fire I've come to adore." His hand tightened on her waist. "And I realized something."

Clara's breath caught. Around them, the crowd had gone completely silent, but she barely noticed. All she could see was him—the way his eyes softened when they met hers, the slight quirk of his lips that he seemed to reserve just for her.

"What did you realize?" she whispered.

"That I'm tired of waiting." His free hand came up to cup her cheek. "That I'm done pretending this is anything less than what it is."

Her heart was hammering so hard she wondered if he could hear it. "And what is it?"

"Love." The word fell from his lips like a confession, like a prayer. "I love you, Clara Romano. Not because you're a noble lady, though you wear the title as if you were born to it. Not because you're the most talented seamstress in London, though your skill takes my breath away."

She couldn't breathe. Couldn't think. Could only stare up at him as he continued.

"I love you because you're you. Because you fight for what you believe in. Because you care more about others than yourself. Because you make me laugh, challenge me, drive me absolutely mad sometimes." His thumb brushed across her cheekbone. "Because somehow, without my permission or planning, you've become essential to me."

Someone in the crowd—it sounded suspiciously like Margaret—let out a delighted squeal. Clara barely heard it over the roaring in her ears.

"I know this isn't how things are usually done," Eustace continued, his lips quirking into that half-smile she loved so much. "But then again, nothing about us has ever been usual, has it?"

And then, right there in the middle of his ballroom, in front of what felt like all of London society, the Duke of Ravencroft kissed her hand.

Clara's hand flew to her mouth. "Eustace—"

"I love you," he said simply, his eyes never leaving hers.

"I love you too, you know."

His smile was blinding. "I know."

And there, the lost girl had finally found her way home.

# Chapter Eighteen

Eustace had never been a man given to public displays of emotion. He had built his reputation on being coolly logical, detached, a man who sneered at the very notion of romantic entanglements.

And yet here he stood, in the middle of London's most prestigious ballroom, about to make the biggest spectacle of himself in the name of love.

He wouldn't have it any other way.

Clara's hand trembled in his as his lips touched the back of it.

The candlelight caught the tears still drying on her cheeks—tears from his earlier confession of love, tears from the night's dramatic revelations. She had never looked more beautiful.

"Clara," he said, his voice carrying in the sudden quiet that had fallen over the ballroom. He could feel the ton's collective gaze upon them, could practically hear the held breath of anticipation.

Her eyes widened. "Eustace, what are you—"

He dropped to one knee.

The gasps that echoed through the ballroom would have amused him any other time. Now, he had eyes only for Clara, whose face had gone pale with shock.

"Your Grace," she whispered, "please don't—not here, not after—"

"Especially here. Especially now." His voice was firm, though his heart thundered in his chest. "I want every person in this room to witness this moment."

"But they know who I am now," she protested softly. "A seamstress and—"

"The bravest, most remarkable woman I have ever known," he cut in, his tone brooking no argument. "And the only woman I will ever want as my duchess."

More gasps, followed by excited whispers. From the corner of his eye, he caught sight of his mother dabbing at her eyes with a handkerchief, his sister beaming beside her. Vittoria stood nearby, her smile radiant as she watched her newfound sister.

"You cannot mean—" Clara's voice shook.

"I absolutely mean it." His grip on her hand tightened. "I, who once swore I would never marry for love, find myself utterly and completely in love with you. Not with a title or a position, but with you, Clara. The woman who challenges me, who makes me laugh, who has turned my entire world upside down and made it infinitely better in the process."

Tears spilled down her cheeks. "Eustace..."

"I love your passion for your craft, your kindness to those others overlook, your fierce determination to make your own way in the world." His voice grew rougher with emotion. "I love that you can reduce me to madness with a single smile, that you're not afraid to argue with me, that you've made me want things I never thought I would."

"Are you sure?" she whispered, her voice barely audible. "Even knowing everything?"

"Knowing everything only makes me more certain." He reached into his pocket, withdrawing a ring that had been burning a hole there all evening. "You were never meant to be just my convenient fake fiancée, Clara. You were meant to be my everything."

The ring caught the light—a perfect sapphire surrounded by diamonds, chosen specifically because it reminded him of the sparkle in her eyes when she was happy.

"Marry me," he said, his voice carrying the authority of his position but softened by love. "Be my duchess, my partner, my love. Let me spend the rest of my life proving that you belong exactly where you are—by my side."

Clara's free hand flew to her mouth, tears flowing freely now. Around them, the ton waited with bated breath.

"Say yes, dear!" His mother's voice rang out, startling a laugh from Clara.

"Please say yes," his sister added, practically bouncing with excitement.

Vittoria stepped forward, taking her sister's other hand. "Say yes, Clara. Let us be a real family at last." Her eyes shimmered with tears. "And perhaps... perhaps you'll come to Italy with us? There are people there who have missed you all their lives, who would give anything to see you again."

Clara looked around at the faces surrounding them—his family, her sister, even the ton who had so recently threatened to condemn her, now watching with romantic enthusiasm. The love and acceptance in their expressions seemed to overwhelm her.

Finally, she looked back at Eustace, still kneeling patiently before her. "You're absolutely certain?" she asked one last time. "Even though I'm not—"

"You're everything," he interrupted firmly. "You're my everything. Now, will you put me out of my misery and answer the question? My knee is beginning to protest."

A laugh bubbled up through her tears. "Yes," she whispered, then louder, "Yes, of course I'll marry you!"

The ballroom erupted in cheers as Eustace slid the ring onto her finger and rose to his feet in one fluid motion. He pulled her into his arms, propriety be damned, and kissed her thoroughly.

"I love you," he murmured against her lips. "My brilliant, maddening, perfect Clara."

She smiled against his mouth. "I love you too, my grumpy, wonderful duke."

Around them, the celebration began in earnest. His mother and sister rushed forward to embrace Clara, while Vittoria beamed through her tears. The orchestra struck up a triumphant tune, and somewhere in the crowd, someone called for more wine.

But Eustace barely noticed any of it. His world had narrowed to the woman in his arms, to the feel of her ring against his chest where her hand rested, to the love shining in her eyes that matched the fierce joy in his own heart.

For the first time in his life, everything was exactly as it should be.

\*\*\*

A WEEK LATER

The journey to Italy began in a carriage, with Clara pressed close to Eustace's side as English countryside rolled past their windows. Vittoria sat across from them, her usual composure somewhat disrupted by the constant jolting of the road.

"I'd forgotten how dreadful English roads could be," she muttered, catching herself against the seat for the third time.

Eustace felt Clara's silent laugh against his shoulder. "The great Countess Romano, undone by a few bumps?"

"A few?" Vittoria's perfectly arched brow rose. "I've seen smoother mountain paths."

It was these moments that fascinated Eustace most—watching the sisters discover each other, seeing how their personalities both clashed and complimented. Where Clara's wit came wrapped in warmth, Vittoria's emerged like a blade from velvet. Yet there was no mistaking the affection beneath their banter.

"Are you certain about this?" Clara whispered later, when Vittoria had dozed off. "Meeting them before the wedding?"

Eustace tightened his arm around her. "Your parents have waited twenty years to see you again. Why make them wait longer?"

"But what if—" She bit her lip. "What if I'm not what they remember? What if I'm too different now?"

"Impossible." He pressed a kiss to her temple. "You're exactly who you're meant to be."

The journey to Dover passed quickly enough, but it was at the harbor that Clara's nerves truly began to show. She stood at the dock, staring up at Eustace's private vessel with wide eyes.

"It's rather large," she managed.

"Only the best for my future duchess," he murmured, guiding her up the gangplank. "And significantly more comfortable than a merchant vessel."

The ship's captain, James Henderson, greeted them with a bow that held just a hint of familiarity. He'd known Eustace since they were boys, after all.

"Your Grace, ladies." His eyes lingered perhaps a moment too long on Vittoria, who suddenly found the ship's rigging fascinating. "Welcome aboard the Lady Anne."

Eustace didn't miss the slight flush that colored Vittoria's cheeks, nor the way Henderson's usual confident stance softened in her presence. *Interesting,* he thought, catching Clara's knowing smile.

The first few days at sea passed in a blur of salt spray and endless horizon. Clara, to everyone's surprise, took to sailing like she'd been born to it. She spent hours on deck, her hair whipping in the wind as she peppered the crew with questions about navigation and sail craft.

"Your sister is quite the natural," Henderson remarked to Vittoria one afternoon, as they watched Clara learn to tie sailor's knots.

"She always did love learning new things," Vittoria replied softly, then seemed startled by her own words—memories she hadn't known she still carried.

Eustace noticed how Henderson's hand moved to steady Vittoria when the ship rolled, how she didn't immediately step away. How his usually proper sister-in-law-to-be seemed to lose some of her rigid poise around the captain.

"I feel like a proud mother." Clara murmured to him later, as they watched Vittoria actually laugh at something Henderson said. "I've been worried about Vittoria being too serious."

"Mmm." Eustace pulled her closer, enjoying the way she fit against him. "Speaking of mothers..."

"Don't." She pressed her face into his coat. "I'm trying not to think about it."

But as they approached the Italian coast, there was no avoiding it any longer. Clara stood at the rail, watching the shoreline emerge from the morning mist. Her hands gripped the wood so tightly her knuckles went white.

"I remember this," she whispered when Eustace joined her. "The way the cliffs look in the sunrise. The smell of the herbs on the breeze." She turned to him, her eyes wide. "How can I remember that?"

"Because it's in your blood," he said simply. "Just as it's in Vittoria's."

The Romano family's carriage met them at the port, grand and gleaming with the family crest. Clara's breath hitched at the sight of it.

The drive to the family estate passed in a blur of stunning vistas and Clara's increasingly rapid breathing. Eustace held her hand throughout, his thumb tracing soothing circles on her skin.

When they crested the final hill and the palazzo came into view, Clara gasped.

"The gardens," she breathed. "The fountain with the mermaids..."

"And that tree—"

"The rose arbor..."

The carriage rolled to a stop before the grand entrance. Through the windows, they could see two figures waiting on the steps—a distinguished gentleman with silver at his temples, and a elegant lady whose hands were clasped tightly together.

Clara's grip on Eustace's hand became almost painful. "I can't—I don't know if I can—"

"You can." He kissed her knuckles. "And I'll be right beside you."

The carriage door opened. Vittoria stepped out first, then turned back with her hand extended. "Come home, sister," she said softly. "Come home at last."

Clara took Vittoria's outstretched hand, her legs trembling as she descended from the carriage.

Clara's hands wouldn't stop shaking, fidgeting with her dress—one she'd made herself, of course. The pale blue silk was perfect for a spring morning, but right now she couldn't stop worrying about whether it was good enough for meeting her real parents.

Her parents. The words still felt strange in her mind.

"Breathe," he murmured. "I'll give you space once I know you're fine."

She tried. She really did. But then the doors opened, and she forgot how.

Eustace's steady presence behind her gave her courage, but nothing could have prepared her for the moment her eyes met those of the couple on the palazzo steps.

The countess moved first, practically flying down the steps with a grace that belied her years. "My baby," she cried in Italian, tears already streaming down her face. "My precious baby girl!"

Clara found herself swept into an embrace so fierce, so full of love, that her knees nearly buckled. Her mother's scent—lavender and something uniquely familiar—enveloped her, and suddenly she was crying too, clinging to this woman who had haunted her dreams for twenty years.

"Mama," she sobbed, the Italian flowing naturally from her lips. "Mama, I remember your scent. I remember—"

"Shh, *tesoro mio*," her mother soothed, pulling back just enough to cup Clara's face in trembling hands. "Let me look at you. Oh, you're so beautiful. So perfect."

The count reached them then, his own tears falling freely. "My child," he breathed, wrapping both his wife and daughter in his arms. "My little nightingale."

The nickname triggered another memory—of sitting on his lap while he told stories, of hiding behind his legs when strangers visited, of feeling absolutely safe in these same strong arms.

"Papa," Clara whispered, turning into his embrace. "I remember... I remember the stories you used to tell. I thought it was all just a dream... I remember the stars and the sea..."

Her father's breath caught on a sob. "You remember?"

Vittoria joined them then, completing their circle. "She remembers more than she knows," she said softly, her own eyes shining. "Just as I remembered her, even when I thought I'd forgotten."

Clara felt overwhelmed by the love surrounding her—her mother's gentle hands still stroking her hair, her father's strong arms holding them all, Vittoria's presence warm and sisterly beside her. And behind them, Eustace, watching with such tenderness it made her heart ache.

"We've been looking for you for so long," her father's voice cracked. "So long..."

Clara couldn't speak. Could barely breathe through her tears. But it didn't matter because they were holding her, murmuring words of love and welcome, and everything felt right.

Until her mother pulled back slightly, her hands framing Clara's face. "My Vittoria."

Clara blinked. "What?"

Her parents exchanged a look that made her stomach drop. Her father cleared his throat. "Perhaps we should sit."

The next few minutes passed in a blur as they made their way inside to the drawing room and settled onto the sofas. Clara's mind was spinning. Something was wrong. Something was—

"You're Vittoria," her mother said softly. "Our firstborn. By three minutes."

Clara stared at her. "But... no. Vittoria is—"

"Vandora," her father supplied gently. "Your twin. When you were taken... we couldn't explain to society that our heir had been stolen. So Vandora became Vittoria."

The room tilted sideways. Clara gripped the edge of the sofa, trying to make sense of it all. "I'm... I'm Vittoria?"

Her mother nodded, tears spilling down her cheeks. "We thought we were protecting both of you. Vandora took your place, and became Vittoria in name, while we searched for you. We never stopped searching."

Clara's head spun. She was Vittoria. The real Vittoria. The one who had been betrothed to Eustace all those years ago. The one who–

Oh lord.

She excused herself from the drawing room, her head spinning as she made her way to the garden. She needed air. And space. And possibly a very large glass of wine, though it was barely noon.

Vittoria followed Clara to the garden and sat on the bench beside her. "You knew?" Clara asked.

"Since I was twelve. I found the papers in Father's study. The real birth records. I had been waiting for the right moment to tell you, but..." She gestured helplessly. "How do you tell someone something like that?"

Clara stared at the roses, their pale pink petals swaying in the breeze. "So all this time, when I was pretending to be you..."

"You were actually pretending to be yourself." Vittoria's laugh held a touch of irony. "Quite the twist, isn't it?"

They sat in silence for a moment, the weight of truth settling between them. Then Vittoria turned to her, her expression uncertain.

"I suppose... well, now that you know, you'll want your name back? It is rightfully yours, after all."

Clara's head snapped up so fast she nearly gave herself whiplash. "What? No! Absolutely not."

"But Clara, it's your birth name, your right—"

"And you've made it yours," Clara cut her off firmly. "Look at you—you're every inch Lady Vittoria Romano. The name suits you perfectly."

"But—"

"No buts." Clara grabbed her sister's hands. "I'm Clara. I've always been Clara, even when I didn't know who I really was. It's who I became, who I chose to be." She squeezed Vittoria's fingers. "And you're Vittoria. That's who you are."

"Are you sure?" Vittoria's voice was small, uncertain. "I've felt guilty for so long, using your name..."

"Well, stop it." Clara bumped her shoulder playfully. "Besides, can you imagine trying to explain to everyone that we're switching names now? The scandal would be ridiculous. Lord Edmund might actually explode this time."

That startled a laugh out of Vittoria. "You're impossible, you know that?"

"So I've been told." Clara grinned. "Usually by Eustace. Speaking of whom..." Her grin faltered slightly. "I should probably go see how my soon-to-be husband is coping with the fact that he has been engaged to the right woman all along."

"Only you," Vittoria shook her head, smiling. "Only you could accidentally impersonate yourself."

Clara stood, brushing off her skirts. "Well, I've never been one for doing things the simple way."

"That's certainly true." Vittoria caught her hand as she turned to go. "Clara? Thank you."

Clara squeezed her hand. "What are sisters for? Even if we did do everything backwards."

***

Clara found Eustace in the study of the room assigned to him, standing by the window with his hands clasped behind his back. The familiar pose made her smile despite her nerves—he always stood like that when he was thinking too hard about something.

"I can hear you worrying from here," she said.

He turned, and the look in his eyes made her breath catch. There was wonder there, and confusion, and something deeper that made her heart race.

"So," she fidgeted with her skirts, "I suppose you are about to marry the right woman after all. Turns out I am Vittoria. Surprise?"

She tried for a light tone, but her voice wobbled. Eustace crossed the room in three long strides, his hands coming up to cup her face.

"That's why," he murmured, his thumb brushing her cheek. "That's why I couldn't go through with it back then. When Vittoria—Vandora—came to Italy. Something felt wrong."

Clara leaned into his touch. "You remembered me?"

"Not consciously. But something in me must have known." His dark eyes searched her face. "I have faint memories of us, you know. Before... before everything."

Eustace pulled her closer, resting his forehead against hers. "When I met you again, that first night at the ball... something about you felt so familiar. Even when I thought you were pretending to be Vittoria, some part of me recognized you."

"Is that why you kept me around?" She couldn't resist teasing. "Some childhood memory?"

"I kept you around because you drove me mad," he growled playfully. "Because you challenged everything I thought I knew. Because you made me feel alive again."

"Sweet talker."

"It's true." His voice softened. "You were never pretending to be someone else, Clara. You were always just being you—the same fierce, brilliant, impossible woman I was meant to love."

Clara's heart felt too big for her chest. "Even when I was just a seamstress?"

"Especially then." He kissed her forehead. "Though I suppose this explains why you have such excellent taste."

She smacked his chest lightly. "Careful, Your Grace. I might start thinking you want to marry me only for my dressmaking skills."

"Never." His expression turned serious. "I want to marry you because you're you. Vittoria or Clara, noble or seamstress—none of that matters. What matters is this." He took her hand and placed it over his heart. "What matters is us."

Clara rose on her tiptoes and hugged him, pouring everything she couldn't say into it. He responded immediately, his arms wrapping around her waist and pulling her closer.

When they finally broke apart, both breathing heavily, Clara couldn't help but smile. "So you're not disappointed? That you accidentally will marry the right woman?"

Eustace laughed, the sound rich and warm. "My love, marrying you is going to be the only thing I've ever done completely right—accident or not."

Clara returned to the drawing room hand-in-hand with Eustace, her heart feeling lighter than it had in years. Her parents—her real parents—sat on the sofa, their hands clasped together, looking anxious but hopeful.

"I'm sorry I ran off," she said, smoothing her skirts as she sat across from them. "I needed a moment to... well, to process everything."

Her mother leaned forward. "We understand, darling. It's a lot to take in."

"It is." Clara took a deep breath. "But I want you to know—both of you—that none of it changes how happy I am to have found you again."

Her father's eyes grew misty. "Even after we failed to protect you?"

"You didn't fail." Clara's voice was firm. "You looked for me. You never gave up. And look—here I am."

Her mother made a small sound, somewhere between a laugh and a sob. "Here you are. Our little girl, all grown up and engaged to the very man you were meant for."

Clara felt Eustace's hand squeeze her shoulder. "About that... Vittoria—I mean, Vandora and I talked. I want her to keep the name."

"Are you sure?" Her father frowned. "It's your birthright—"

"My birthright is having a family who loves me," Clara interrupted gently. "And I have that now. I don't need a different name to prove who I am."

Her mother rose from the sofa and came to sit beside her, taking Clara's hands in hers. "You always were the stubborn one. Even as a baby." She touched Clara's cheek softly. "You used to scrunch up your nose just like that when you'd made up your mind about something."

Clara laughed wetly. "Some things never change, I suppose."

"Tell me everything," her mother said suddenly. "Everything I've missed. Every moment, every triumph, every tear. I want to know all of it."

"That might take a while."

"We have time," her father said, moving to join them. "All the time in the world."

So Clara told them. About growing up, about discovering her talent with a needle and thread, about building her business from nothing. Her mother cried when she described the lonely nights, and her father's hands clenched when she mentioned her stepfather's cruelty. But they also laughed at her tales of demanding customers and beamed with pride when she showed them her designs.

"And now look at you," her mother said hours later, as the sun began to set outside. "A successful businesswoman, a duchess, and still so completely, wonderfully yourself."

"You don't mind?" Clara bit her lip. "That I want to keep working? That I'm not quite the proper lady I should be?"

Her father laughed. "Mind? My dear, you're exactly who you were always meant to be. Noble blood or not, you've made your own way in the world. We couldn't be prouder."

Clara felt tears threatening again. "I've cried more today than I have in years."

"Happy tears," her mother said, wiping her own eyes. "The very best kind."

"Speaking of happy things," Clara's father cleared his throat, looking suspiciously misty-eyed himself. "Your mother and I have something for you."

He pulled out a small package wrapped in silk. Clara opened it carefully to find a leather-bound journal, its pages filled with her mother's elegant handwriting.

"Every day," her mother explained softly. "Every day since you were taken, I wrote to you. Everything I wished I could tell you, everything I hoped you'd know someday."

Clara traced the pages with trembling fingers. "Mama..."

"Your Grace," her father called to Eustace, his voice rough with emotion. "Come. Join your family."

As Eustace stepped forward, Clara saw her mother's eyes widen with fresh tears. "You brought her back to us," the countess said, reaching for his hand. "You found our lost girl and brought her home."

"She found herself," Eustace corrected gently, his hand settling warm and steady on Clara's back. "I merely had the good fortune to be there when she did."

They stood together on the sun-warmed steps, crying and laughing and holding each other. Clara's mother couldn't seem to stop touching her face, her hair, her hands, as though ensuring she was real. Her father kept whispering "my girls, my precious girls" in Italian, while Vittoria maintained her own grip on Clara's hand.

"Come, let's eat. Celebrate," her mother finally said, though she made no move to release Clara. "Come home, *tesoro*. Come see where you belong."

As they turned toward the palazzo's grand entrance, Clara felt Eustace squeeze her hand. Looking up at him, she saw all the love and pride and joy she felt reflected in his eyes.

She was home. Not just to the palazzo of her birth, but to the family who had never stopped loving her, never stopped searching. To the sister who completed her heart, and to the man who had helped her find her way back to herself.

She was, at last, exactly where she belonged.

# Chapter Nineteen

A month after their return to England, Eustace stood at the altar of St. George's Chapel, trying not to let show how his heart thundered against his ribs. The chapel glowed with hundreds of candles, their light catching on the Italian silk flowers Clara had personally crafted for the occasion—a perfect blend of her two worlds.

He had once sworn he would never stand here, never bind himself in marriage. Now he could barely contain his impatience to see his bride.

When the chapel doors opened, everything else faded away.

Clara stood with her father—the Count Romano. But it was her dress that drew every eye in the chapel.

She had designed and sewn it herself, of course. Ivory silk that seemed to float as she walked, with delicate embroidery that told their story in thread—tiny masks for their first meeting, roses from the Romano gardens, even a small ship for their journey home. The Italian lace veil had been her mother's, and around her neck lay both her childhood locket and the sapphire pendant Eustace had given her.

She was radiant. Perfect. His.

Their eyes met across the chapel, and Eustace felt his carefully maintained composure crack. Clara's smile grew wider at whatever she saw in his face, her own eyes bright with tears.

The ceremony passed in a blur of ancient words and newer promises. When asked for their vows, Eustace spoke first, his voice carrying clearly through the hushed chapel.

"I once thought love was a weakness," he said, holding Clara's trembling hands in his. "You proved me wrong in every way possible. You challenged me, surprised me, and made me want things I never thought I would. I vow to spend every day showing you that you belong exactly where you are—by my side, as my duchess, my partner, and my heart."

Clara's tears spilled over as she began her own vows. "I spent so long pretending to be someone else, never knowing I was searching for myself. You saw me—the real me—even before I knew who that was. I vow to love you with all that I am, all that I was, and all that I will become."

When they were pronounced man and wife, Eustace pulled her close and kissed her with all the passion he usually kept carefully controlled. The chapel erupted in cheers and happy tears.

Later, at their wedding breakfast, Clara danced with her father while Eustace watched with uncharacteristic softness in his expression. Vittoria caught his eye from where she stood with Captain Henderson, her own smile knowing.

But it was the quiet moments Eustace treasured most—Clara's hand in his as they greeted guests, her quiet laugh against his shoulder as they danced, the way she leaned into him when she grew tired.

As evening fell and the celebration continued, Eustace led his bride away from the crowds. They slipped through the quiet corridors of

Ravencroft House until they reached their chambers—her old room now joined with his into a private sanctuary.

Clara's hand trembled in his as they crossed the threshold. The room glowed with firelight and scattered candles, rose petals strewn across the massive bed.

"Nervous?" he asked softly, drawing her into his arms.

She nodded against his chest. "A little. But not afraid." She looked up at him, trust shining in her eyes. "Never afraid with you."

Eustace kissed her then, pouring all his love and tenderness into it. His hands moved to the tiny buttons of her wedding gown—buttons he knew she had sewn herself—undoing each one with reverent care.

"I love you," he murmured against her skin. "My brilliant, beautiful wife."

Clara's fingers worked at his cravat, her touch both shy and determined. "I love you too," she whispered. "My grumpy, wonderful husband."

They took their time, learning each other with gentle touches and whispered words of love. Eustace worshipped every inch of her, showing with actions what he sometimes struggled to say with words. Clara bloomed under his attention, her initial shyness giving way to passion that matched his own.

Later, as they lay tangled in silk sheets, Clara traced idle patterns on his chest. "Thank you," she murmured.

"For what, my love?"

"For seeing me. The real me. For making me feel like I belong."

Eustace pulled her closer, pressing a kiss to her temple. "You've always belonged here. It just took us both a while to realize it."

Clara smiled against his skin, and Eustace felt the last piece of his world slide perfectly into place. Here, with his wife in his arms and their future stretching bright before them, he was exactly where he was meant to be.

They fell asleep wrapped in each other's arms, their wedding rings glinting in the dying firelight—a duke who had learned to love, and a seamstress who had found her true self in the most unexpected way possible.

It was, in every way, their perfect beginning.

**A MONTH LATER**

A month later, Clara stood in the glittering ballroom of Ravencroft House, watching the dancers whirl by in a blur of color and movement. Her own gown—a creation she was particularly proud of—sparkled in the candlelight, the deep purple silk making her feel like royalty.

Which, technically, she supposed she was now. Sort of.

The thought made her giggle, though she quickly pressed her hand to her mouth to stifle it. She'd been feeling oddly giddy all evening, her head spinning pleasantly even though she hadn't touched a drop of wine.

"Something amusing, Duchess?"

She turned to find Eustace watching her with that look that still made her knees weak—as if she was the most fascinating thing he'd ever seen.

"Just thinking about how ridiculous life is," she said, reaching for him. But as she moved, the room tilted sideways.

"Clara?" Eustace's voice sharpened with concern as he caught her elbow.

"I'm fine," she said automatically, though the room wouldn't stop spinning. "Just a bit... oh."

The world went dark.

When she opened her eyes again, she was in her bedroom, with Eustace's worried face hovering above her. His eyes were suspiciously red-rimmed.

"Welcome back," he said softly, his hand squeezing hers.

"What happened?"

"You fainted." His voice was rough. "Scared about ten years off my life."

Clara tried to sit up, but he pressed her gently back against the pillows. "The doctor's already been," he said, and something in his tone made her heart skip.

"And?"

A smile broke across his face—the kind she'd only seen once before, on their wedding day. "And it seems, my love, that we're going to have a baby."

Clara's hands flew to her stomach. "What?"

"A baby," he repeated, his eyes shining. "Our baby."

"But... how?"

He arched an eyebrow. "Well, when a duke and duchess love each other very much..."

"Oh, hush!" She smacked his arm, but she was laughing, tears of joy spilling down her cheeks. "A baby. We're having a baby!"

"We are." He leaned down to kiss her, his hand covering hers where it rested on her stomach. "Though I must insist you stop fainting to tell me important news. My heart can't take it."

"I'll try my best." She pulled him down for another kiss, then froze. "Oh! We have to tell everyone! My parents, and Vittoria, and your mother—oh lord, your mother's going to be impossible..."

"Already taken care of," he murmured against her hair. "Though I think Margaret might actually expire from excitement."

Clara laughed, feeling like her heart might burst with happiness. "I love you," she whispered. "So much."

"I love you too." His hand stroked her cheek. "Both of you."

She caught his hand, pressing it more firmly against her still-flat stomach. Their baby. A little piece of both of them, growing beneath her heart.

"You know what this means, don't you?" she said after a moment, her eyes twinkling.

"What?"

"I'm going to have to design an entirely new wardrobe."

Eustace's laugh echoed through the room. "Only you, my love," he said fondly. "Only you would think about fashion at a time like this."

"Well, I can hardly let our baby's mother walk around looking anything less than perfect."

"You're always perfect." He kissed her forehead. "Even when you're driving me mad."

"Especially then," she corrected, snuggling into his arms.

As she drifted off to sleep, surrounded by her husband's warmth and the knowledge of the new life growing inside her, Clara couldn't help but smile. From lost child to successful seamstress to duchess to mother—her life had taken more twists and turns than she could count.

But every single one had led her right where she was meant to be.

# Chapter Twenty

Six Months Later

The autumn breeze carried the scent of roses through the open windows of Ravencroft House, making the delicate lace curtains dance. Clara sat at her workbench in her private studio—a wedding gift from Eustace—surrounded by swatches of silk and half-finished designs.

Her hands, usually so steady with a needle, rested on her swollen belly as another kick made her smile.

"Already as restless as your father," she murmured, rubbing gentle circles on her stomach.

"I heard that," Eustace's voice came from the doorway, warm with amusement.

Clara turned to find her husband leaning against the frame, his usual stern expression softened by the look he reserved for her. In the year since their wedding, he had mellowed somewhat—though he still terrorized the ton when they deserved it.

"You were meant to," she teased, holding out her hand to him. "Your son has been practicing his fencing moves all morning."

"Son?" Eustace crossed the room to kneel beside her chair, placing his large hand over hers on her belly. "You seem very certain."

"Mother's intuition." She ran her free hand through his dark hair. "Though Vittoria insists it's a girl."

The mention of her sister made them both smile. Vittoria had married Captain Henderson six months ago in a ceremony that combined English naval tradition with Italian nobility. She now split her time between London and the sea, her once-perfect composure transformed into something wilder and happier.

"Speaking of family," Eustace said, pressing a kiss to her stomach before standing, "your parents' letter arrived this morning. They'll be here in time for the birth."

Clara's eyes brightened. In the past year, she had grown closer to her birth family, their love healing wounds she hadn't known she carried. Her mother had spent months teaching her family recipes and sharing stories of her childhood, while her father had given her journals he'd kept during their years of separation.

"And what about your mother?" she asked, knowing how the Dowager Duchess had taken to visiting daily since Clara's pregnancy was announced.

"Already in the morning room, planning the nursery for the fourth time this week." His tone was exasperated but fond.

Clara laughed, the sound turning to a gasp as the baby kicked again. Eustace's hands were immediately on her, his face concerned.

"I'm fine," she assured him, placing his palm where their child moved. "Perfect, actually."

His expression softened as he felt the movement. "You are, you know," he murmured.

"What?"

"Perfect." He leaned down to kiss her, gentle but thorough. "My perfect duchess."

Clara smiled against his lips. "Still grumpy, I see."

"Only with everyone else." His hand cradled her cheek. "Never with you."

They stayed like that for a moment, basking in their happiness. Clara's workroom had become a sanctuary of sorts—a place where she could be both Duchess and designer, where she created gowns for charity and taught young seamstresses her craft.

"Your Grace?" A maid appeared at the door, bobbing a curtsy. "The Dowager Duchess asks if you'll join her to review the nursery colors. Again."

Eustace groaned, making Clara laugh. "Go," she said, pushing him gently. "Keep your mother from turning our entire house pink. I'll join you shortly."

He stole another kiss before straightening. "Don't work too long. Doctor's orders."

"Yes, My Lord Duke," she said with mock solemnity, then ruined it by winking at him.

As Eustace left to deal with his mother's enthusiasm, Clara turned back to her designs. Her fingers traced the pattern she was creating—a christening gown that combined Romano family tradition with English styling. Perfect for a child born of both worlds.

Her other hand rested on her stomach, feeling the life growing within. A year ago, she had been a seamstress hiding behind a mask. Now she was a duchess, a sister, a daughter restored, and soon to be a mother.

And she had never been happier.

***

"Push, *mi tesoro*!" the Countess Romano urged, gripping Clara's hand as another contraction seized her. "Just like that!"

Clara had been in labor for six hours, surrounded by both her mothers—the countess holding one hand, her stepmother the other. Outside, Eustace wore a path in the carpet, flanked by her father who tried in vain to calm him.

"One more," the midwife called. "One more big push, Your Grace!"

Clara gathered her remaining strength, squeezing her mothers' hands. With a final, tremendous effort, she pushed—and the room filled with the strong, healthy cry of a newborn.

"A girl!" the midwife announced jubilantly. "A beautiful, perfect girl!"

Tears streamed down Clara's face as they placed her daughter in her arms. The baby had Eustace's dark hair but Clara's delicate features. When she opened her eyes, they were the same striking blue shared by Clara and Vittoria.

"Let him in," Clara whispered, unable to take her eyes off her daughter. "Let him see her."

Eustace practically burst through the door, his usual composure completely abandoned. He stopped short at the sight of them, his eyes wide with wonder.

"Clara," he breathed, crossing to the bed in two long strides. "My love..."

"Come meet your daughter," she said softly, shifting so he could see the baby's face. "She has your hair."

Eustace sat carefully on the edge of the bed, reaching out with trembling fingers to touch their daughter's tiny hand. The baby immediately gripped his finger, and Clara saw tears fill her husband's eyes.

"She's perfect," he whispered. "Just like her mother."

Their families crowded around, exclaiming over the baby's features—the Romano eyes, the Montague chin, the perfect blend of both bloodlines.

"What will you call her?" Vittoria asked from where she stood with her own husband, her hand resting on her slightly rounded stomach.

Clara exchanged a look with Eustace before answering. "Margaret Rose," she said. "Margaret for your mother, and Rose..."

"For the garden where you first met," her father finished, understanding dawning in his eyes.

"And where we found each other again," Eustace added softly, pressing a kiss to Clara's temple.

Little Margaret chose that moment to yawn, drawing coos from both grandmothers. Clara felt her heart might burst with love—for her daughter, her husband, this beautiful family that had grown from loss into something more precious than she could have imagined.

"I love you," Eustace murmured against her hair. "Both of you. More than I ever thought possible."

Clara leaned into him, their daughter cradled between them. "And I love you, my grumpy duke. Thank you for seeing me, even when I was hiding."

"Always," he promised.

Later, when the excitement had calmed and their families had withdrawn to let them rest, Clara sat in the nursery's window seat with Margaret at her breast. Eustace stood behind them, one hand on Clara's shoulder, the other gently stroking their daughter's dark curls.

The sunset painted the gardens in shades of gold, highlighting the roses that had started their story. In the distance, they could hear the happy chatter of their family—English and Italian voices blending in harmony.

"Happy?" Eustace asked softly.

Clara looked up at him, then down at their daughter, thinking of how far they'd come. From a masked ball to this moment, from deception to the deepest truth, from two broken people to a family made whole.

"Perfect," she answered, and meant it with all her heart.

For this was their happily ever after—a duke who had learned to love, a seamstress who had found herself, and the little princess who represented all their dreams come true.

And they lived happily ever after, indeed.

## THE END

**Thank you for reading "Clara, Stitched In Secrets."**

**If you loved this book, you will love the first book in my Somersley Series Entitled "Governess Penelope and a Duke!"**

*It's a feel-good story about an unexpected second chance with a first love.*

Click here and get your FREE copy of "Governess Penelope and a Duke": https://dl.bookfunnel.com/a5l15u9hpa

In 1811 London, Penelope, a governess disowned by her father, discovers love while preparing her friend's niece for society.

*This full-length second-chance romance offers a happily-ever-after ending,*

Click here and get your FREE copy of Governess Penelope and a Duke now! https://dl.bookfunnel.com/a5l15u9hpa

PLEASE LEAVE A REVIEW FOR "Clara, Stitched In Secrets".

Made in United States
North Haven, CT
11 January 2025